Young Lord Stranleigh: A Novel

Robert Barr

ESPRIOS DIGITAL PUBLISHING

YOUNG LORD STRANLEIGH

A Novel

By Robert Barr

Illustrated

New York: D. Appleton And Company

1908

YOUNG LORD STRANLEIGH

ROBERT BARR

"The enraged captive . . turned round, his face ablaze with anger."

[Page 78.]

Young Lord Stranleigh

A NOVEL

By

ROBERT BARR

Author of "The Measure of the Rule," "The Triumphs of Eugene Valmont," etc.

ILLUSTRATED

NEW YORK
D. APPLETON AND COMPANY
1908

CONTENTS

CHAPTER I—THE KING'S MOVE IN THE CITY

IT was shortly after nine o'clock in the morning that young Lord Stranleigh of Wychwood, in a most leisurely fashion, descended the front steps of his town house into the street. The young man was almost too perfectly dressed. Every article of his costume, from his shiny hat to the polished boots, was so exactly what it should he, that he ran some danger of being regarded as a model for one of those beautiful engravings of well-dressed mankind which decorate the shops of Bond-Street tailors. He was evidently one who did no useful work in the world, and as a practical person might remark, why should he, when his income was more than thirty thousand pounds a year? The slightly bored expression of his countenance, the languid droop of his eyelids, the easy but indifferent grace of motion that distinguished him, might have proclaimed to a keen observer that the young man had tested all things, and found there was nothing worth getting excited about. He was evidently a person without enthusiasm, for even the sweet perfection of his attire might be attributed to the thought and care of his tailor, rather than to any active meditation on his own part. Indeed, his indolence of attitude made the very words "active" or "energetic" seem superfluous in our language. His friends found it difficult, if not impossible, to interest Lord Stranleigh in anything, even in a horse race, or the fling of the dice, for he possessed so much more money than he needed, that gain or loss failed to excite a passing flutter of emotion. If he was equipped with brains, as some of his more intimate friends darkly hinted, he had hitherto given no evidence of the fact. Although well set up, he was not an athlete. He shot a little, hunted a little, came to town during the season, went to the Continent when the continental exodus took place, always doing the conventional thing, but not doing it well enough or bad enough to excite comment. He was the human embodiment of the sentiment: "There is nothing really worth while."

In marked contrast to him stood, undecided, a man of his own age, with one foot on the lower stone step which led up to the front door of his lordship's town house. His clothes, of undistinguished cut, were worn so carelessly that they almost gave the impression of being ready-made. His flung-on, black slouch hat suggested Western America or Southern Africa. His boots were coarse and clumsy.

But if the attire was uninspiring, the face merited, and usually received, a second glance. It was smooth-shaven, massive and strong, tanned to a slight mahogany tinge by a more eager sun than ever shines on England. The eyes were deep, penetrating, determined, masterful.

Lord Stranleigh's delicate upper lip supported a silken mustache carefully tended; his eyes were languid and tired, capable of no such gleam of intensity as was now turned upon him from the eyes of the other.

"I beg your pardon, sir, but are you Lord Stranleigh of Wychwood?"

His lordship paused on the upper steps, and drawled the one word "Yes."

"My name is Peter Mackeller, and the Honorable John Hazel gave me a letter of introduction to you, saying I should probably catch you in at this hour. It seems he underestimated your energy, for you are already abroad."

There was an undercurrent of resentment in the impatient tone Mackeller had used. He was manifestly impressed unfavorably by this modern representative of a very ancient family, but the purpose he had in view caused him to curb his dislike, although he had not been tactful enough to prevent a hint of it appearing in his words. If the other had gathered any impression of that hint, he was too perfectly trained to betray his knowledge, either in phrase or expression of countenance. The opinion of his fellows was a matter of complete indifference to him. A rather engaging smile stirred the silken mustache.

"Oh, Jack always underestimates my good qualities, so we won't trouble about his note of introduction. Besides, a man cannot read a letter in the street, can he?"

"I see no reason against it," replied the other sharply.

"Don't you really? Well, I am going across to my club, and perhaps as we walk along together, you will be good enough to say why you wish to see me."

Lord Stranleigh was about to proceed down another step when the other answered "No" so brusquely that his lordship paused once more, with a scarcely perceptible elevation of the eyebrows, for, as a rule, people did not say "No" to Lord Stranleigh of Wychwood, who was known to enjoy thirty thousand pounds a year.

"Then what do you propose?" asked his lordship, as though his own suggestion had exhausted all the possibilities of action.

"I propose that you open the door, invite me in, and give me ten minutes of your valuable time."

The smile on his lordship's countenance visibly increased.

"That's not a bad idea," he said, with the air of one listening to unexpected originality. "Won't you come in, Mr. Mackeller?" and with his latchkey he opened the door, politely motioning the other to precede him.

Young Mackeller was ushered into a small room to the left of the hall. It was most severely plain, paneled somberly in old oak, lit by one window, and furnished with several heavy leather-covered chairs. In the center stood a small table, carrying a huge bottle of ink, like a great dab of black metal which had been flung while soft on its surface, and now, hardened, sat broad and squat as if it were part of the table itself. On a mat lay several pens, and at one end of the table stood a rack such as holds paper and envelopes, but in this case of most minute proportions, displaying three tiers, one above the other, of what appeared to be visiting cards; twelve minute compact packs all in all, four in each row.

"This," said Lord Stranleigh, with almost an air of geniality, "is my business office."

The visitor looked around him. There were no desks; no pillars of drawers; no japanned-metal boxes that held documents; no cupboards; no books; no pictures.

"Pray be seated, Mr. Mackeller," and when the young man had accepted the invitation, Lord Stranleigh drew up opposite to him at the small table with the packets of cards close to his right hand.

"And now, if you will oblige me with Jack's letter, I will glance over it, though he rarely writes anything worth reading."

Mackeller handed him the letter in an open envelope. His lordship slowly withdrew the document, adjusted an eyeglass, and read it; then he returned it to the envelope, and passed it back to its owner.

"Would it be too much if I asked you to replace it in your pocket, as there is no waste-paper basket in this room?"

Mackeller acted as requested, but the frown on his broad brow deepened. This butterfly seemed to annoy him with his imperturbable manner, and his trifling, finicky, childish insincerity. Confronted with a real man, Mackeller felt he might succeed, but he had already begun to fear that this bit of mental thistle-down would evade him, so instead of going on with his recital, he sat there glowering at Lord Stranleigh, who proved even more of a nonentity than the Honorable John Hazel had led him to believe. He had been prepared to meet some measure of irresponsible inanity, but not quite so much as this. It was Lord Stranleigh himself who broke the silence.

"What do you want?" he asked, almost as if some of his opponent's churlishness had hypnotically permeated into his own being.

"Money," snapped the other shortly.

"Ah, they all do," sighed his lordship, once more a picture of indolent nonchalance.

He selected from the rack beside him four cards, one from each of the little packs in the lower range. These he spread face upward on the table before him.

"I never trouble about money," said his lordship, smiling.

"You probably don't need to, with thirty thousand a year," suggested Mackeller.

"Ah, that's exaggerated," explained his lordship. "You forget the beastly income tax. Still, I was not referring to the amount; I merely wished to explain my methods of dealing with it. Here are the names and addresses of four eminent solicitor persons in the city. There is little use of my keeping four dogs and barking myself, is there? I've really twelve dogs altogether, as represented in this cardcase, but one or other of these four will doubtless suit our purpose. Now, this firm of solicitors attends to one form of charity."

"I don't want charity," growled Mackeller.

"Quite so. I am merely explaining. This firm attends to all the charities that are recognized in our set; the hospitals, the—well whatever they happen to be. When applied to personally in these matters, I write my name on the card of these solicitors, and forward it. Application is then made to them. They look into the matter, and save me the fatigue of investigation. The next firm"—holding up a second card—"deals with charities that are our of our purview; halfdays at the seaside, and that sort of thing. Now I come to business. This firm"—showing the third card—"looks after permanent investments, while this"—lifting the fourth—"takes charge of anything which is speculative in its nature. The applicant receives the particular card which pertains to his particular line of desire. He calls upon the estimable firm of solicitors, and either convinces them, or fails: gets his money, or doesn't. So you see, my affairs are competently transacted, and I avoid the emotional strain of listening to explanations which probably I have not the mental grasp of business to understand. Now, which of these four cards may I have the pleasure of autographing for you?"

"Not one of them, my lord," replied Mackeller. "The Honorable John Hazel said that if you would listen to me, he thought I might interest you."

"Oh, impossible," drawled his lordship, sitting back languidly in his chair.

"Yes, he said it would be a hard task, but I am accustomed to difficulties. I asked you, as we came in, to give me ten minutes. Will you do it?"

"Why," protested his lordship, "we have already spent ten minutes at least."

"Yes, fooling with cards."

"Ah, I'm more accustomed to handling cards than listening to a financial conversation; not these kind of cards, either."

"Will you, for the sake of John Hazel, who tells me he is a friend of yours, give me ten minutes more of your time?"

"What has Jack Hazel to do with this? Are you going to share with him? Is he setting you on to me for loot, and then do you retire into a dark corner, and divide? Jack Hazel's always short of money."

"No, we don't divide, my lord. Mr. Hazel has been speculating in the city, and he stands to win a bit if I can pull off what I'm trying to do. So, if you agree to my proposal, he will prove a winner, so will I, so will you, for you will share in the profits."

"Oh, but I don't need the money."

"Well, we do."

"So I understand. Why doesn't Jack confine himself to the comparative honesty of the dice? What does he want to muddle about in the city for?"

"I suppose because he hasn't got thirty thousand a year."

"Very likely; very likely. Yes, that strikes me as a sufficient explanation. All right, Mr. Mac-keller, take your ten minutes, and try to make your statement as simple as possible. I hope statistics do not come into it. I've no head for figures."

"My father," began the young man, with blunt directness, "is a stockbroker in the city. The firm is Mackeller and Son. I am the son."

"You don't look to me like a stockbroker. That is, what I've always expected such a person to be: I've never met one."

"No, I'm in reality a mining engineer."

"But, my dear sir, you have just said you were a stockbroker."

"I said my father was."

"You said Mackeller and Son, and that you were the son."

"Yes, I am a partner in the firm, but, nevertheless, a mining engineer."

"Do stockbrokers make mining engineers of their sons?"

"One of them did. My father is a rigidly honest man, and preferred me to be an engineer." His lordship's eyebrows again elevated themselves.

"An honest man and a stockbroker? Ah, you *do* interest me, in spite of my pessimism."

"The great difficulty," went on Mackeller, unheeding, "is to obtain an honest estimate of the real value of any distant mining property which is offered for sale in London. There has never been a mining swindle floated on the public which has not had engineer's reports by men of high standing, showing it to possess a value which after events proved quite unreliable. So my father made me a mining engineer, and before he touches any property of this nature, or advises his clients to invest, he compels the promoters to send me out to the mine, and investigate."

"I see," said his lordship, with almost a glimmer of comprehension in his eyes. "Rather a shrewd old man, I take it. He protects himself and his customers, provides a good livelihood for you, his son, and that at the expense of the promoters. Excellent. Go on."

For the first time young Peter Mackeller smiled. "Yes," he said, "my father is very shrewd. He comes from the North, but for once he has got nipped, and the next few hours will decide whether the accumulations of a lifetime are swept away or not. Indeed," he continued, glancing at his watch, "that will be decided within eight minutes, depending on whether I interest you or not."

"Continue," commanded his lordship.

"Early in the year a property called the Red Shallows, situated in West Africa, was brought to him by a syndicate of seven men, able, but somewhat unscrupulous financiers. Their story appeared incredible on its face, for it was no less than that the gold was on the surface, in estimated value a thousand times the amount for which they wished the company formed. They wished my father to underwrite the company for a hundred thousand pounds, and they stipulated that the shares should be sold, not by public subscription, but taken up privately among my father's clients. Afterwards, when the value of the property was fully proved, there would be an immense flotation running into millions, and the profit of this my father was to share."

"Pardon my interruption," said his lordship.

"If what these men stated was true, why didn't they send some one with a basket, and gather the gold they needed, without going to any stockbroker and sharing with him."

"That, my lord, is practically what my father thought, although, of course, he did not believe a word of their story. Still, he understood that these men were not mine magnates in the proper sense of the word; they were merely financiers, speculators, who did not wish to wait for the full development of their property, but simply intended, so they said, to go as far as was necessary to convince the public that this was an even bigger thing than the wealthiest mine of the Rand, and so loot their gold, not from the bosom of the earth, but from the pockets of the British public; but, as I have said, he did not believe a word of their story. However, he made the usual proviso that they should send me out there, and the seven men instantly placed in his hands the necessary amount for my expenses, and I sailed away."

"Why should sane financiers spend good money when they knew they would be found out if they were not telling the truth?"

"Well, my lord, that thought occurred to both my father and myself. I reasoned it out in this way. These seven men had acquired the goldfields from a party of explorers, or from a single explorer, who had discovered it. They probably paid very little money to the discoverer, perhaps not buying it outright, but merely securing an option. Whoever had parted with his rights had evidently succeeded in convincing the syndicate that he spoke the truth. Whether the syndicate hadn't sufficient capital to develop the property, or preferred to risk other people's cash in opening the mine, I do not know, but they evidently thought it worth while to spend some of their own money and send me out there, that they might receive an independent and presumably honest opinion on its value. Be that as it may, there was no exposure forthcoming. The property proved even richer than they had stated. It so seldom happens in the city that anything offered for sale greatly exceeds in value the price asked for it, that the members of the syndicate were themselves surprised when they read my report. It had been arranged, and the document signed before I left England, that my father should get for them not less than fifty thousand pounds nor more than a hundred thousand, for working capital to send out an expedition, buy machinery, and so forth. Now, however, the syndicate proposed that the company should be formed for something like a million pounds. My father pointed out to them the impossibility of getting this sum, for the property was in a locality not hitherto known as a gold-bearing region. Then again, my own standing as a mining engineer carried no particular weight. Although my father believed implicitly in my reports, I was so lacking in celebrity in my profession, it would be folly to attempt to raise any considerable sum on my unsupported word, and rather unsafe to make this discovery public by sending out more eminent engineers. Besides, as I have said, the papers were all signed and stamped, and my father, having a good deal of northern stubbornness in his nature, insisted on the project being carried out as originally projected, so the syndicate was compelled to postpone its onslaught upon the purse of the public.

"My father's compensation was to be a large allotment of paid-up shares in the company, but in addition to this, so great was his faith in my report he himself subscribed, and paid for stock to an extent that rather narrowed his resources. However, his bank agreed, the manager knowing him well, to advance money on his Red Shallows as soon as they had received a quotation on the Stock Exchange.

"The flotation was carried out successfully, my father's friends subscribing largely on his mere word that Red Shallows was a good thing. Only fifty thousand pounds' worth of shares were sold, that being considered enough to purchase the machinery, and send out men in a chartered steamer, with materials for the erection of whatever buildings and appliances as were supposed to be necessary. The rest of the stock was held by the syndicate, with the exception of the amount allotted to my father as compensation for his work. I was to have been appointed engineer of the mine, and had gone to Southampton to charter a suitable steamer, when suddenly an attack was opened upon the new company. Several of the financial papers led this attack, saying that the public had been grossly misled; that there was no gold or other minerals within hundreds of miles of the spot, and that all who had invested in the venture would lose their money. Immediately after this the syndicate dumped its shares on the market, and their price went down with a run."

"Wait a moment," interrupted his lordship. "I think I have given you more than the promised ten minutes, but I believe I have been able to follow you up to the present point. Now, I should like to ask a question or two. Didn't the seven men know that throwing their shares on the market would lower the price?"

"Oh, they knew it perfectly well."

"Then why should they wish to disparage their own property?"

"To freeze out my father and his friends."

"How could they do that if your father and his friends refused to sell?"

"As a matter of fact many of my father's friends have sold. They became frightened, and preferred to lose part rather than the whole. You see, my father had placed every security he possessed into the bank, but with the persistent pounding down of the stock it's going lower and lower every day; in fact, it is unsalable at the present moment. The bank has called upon him to put in further securities, or cash, otherwise it will sell all his possessions for what they will bring."

"But in ruining your father, does not this syndicate ruin itself?"

"No. The financiers have held their annual meeting, appointed a president, board of directors, and all that, and this board is securely in office for a year. As soon as my father and his friends are wiped out the syndicate will quietly buy back the stock at a much lower price than that at which they sold it, and even in crushing my father they will have made a pot of money for themselves."

"Killing two birds with one stone, eh? Isn't there such a thing as gratitude in the City at all?"

"I fear, my lord, there isn't very much of it."

"What amount of money do you need to protect your father's stock?"

"I think five thousand pounds would do."

"I don't pretend to know much about business, Mr. Mackeller, but it seems to me that would merely be the thin end of the wedge. Suppose they keep on, and lower the price of stock still further? Should not I need to put a second five thousand pounds into your hands to protect the first?"

"That is true, Lord Stranleigh, but I don't see how the shares can go much lower than they are. They closed yesterday at two and nine per one-pound share. But in any case the bank will stand by my father if it can. The manager believes in him, although this official, of course, must look after his own employers, but the very fact that my father can put in five thousand pounds this morning will do much to maintain his credit with the manager, and within a very few days we will have time to turn round. I have already seen one or two financiers, and told them what the property is, but they are city-wise, and shake their heads at what they regard as an attempt to unload upon them. So I went to Mr. Hazel, and asked him for an introduction to some one who was rich, and who knew nothing of the ways of the city."

For the first time during the interview, his lordship leaned back and laughed a little.

"You are playing on my ignorance, then?"

"No, I thought perhaps I could get you to believe me."

His lordship did not say whether he believed him or not, but he pressed a button underneath the desk, and there entered to him a solemn-faced man, who stood like a statue, awaiting orders.

"Perkins, will you bring me four check books?"

"Yes, my lord."

"And, Perkins, tell Henri to be at the door with my red automobile within six minutes."

"Yes, my lord."

The man departed, and returned a few moments later, placing on the desk four very thin check books, finally retiring as noiselessly as he had entered.

"An ordinary check book," said his lordship to Mackeller, "does so distort one's coat when placed in an inside pocket, that I cause my books to be made with only one check each inside. I shall now write you out one for five thousand pounds, so that I shall not need to carry its cover with me."

With great leisureliness the young man wrote out a check, tore it from its attachment, and handed it to Mackeller.

"I lend this to you, but I don't think it will be of the slightest use, you know."

"I am quite positive it will protect my father's stock, my lord, and as I am sure that stock will be worth a hundred sovereigns on the pound, if you will accept half my father's holding for this check, I can promise you this will be the biggest day's work you've ever done."

"Ah, that wouldn't be saying very much. Of course, as I told you, I don't pretend to understand business, but where the weak point in your defense lies seems to be in this. Your seven wise men have a year to play about in. I think you said the president and board of directors had been elected only the other day?"

"Yes, my lord, that is so."

"Very well, don't you see they have nearly twelve months during which they can still further press down your stock. The bank will tire of holding what they consider worthless securities, and unless your father can get enough money to redeem all that he has placed in the bank, this five thousand will not even prove a stop-gap."

"I don't agree with your lordship. You see, I shall now keep hammering away on my side. I shall print my report, and post it to every big financier in the city. I shall tell the whole sordid story of this syndicate's action."

"People won't believe you, Mackeller."

"A great many will not, but several may, and these will say 'The stock is so cheap, we might as well take a flutter on a quantity of it.' Then the members of the syndicate are shrewd enough to know that they will excite curiosity, and that some other engineer may be sent out to the property. No, I am convinced that if they do not manage to ruin my father before the end of next week, they will never risk what they now know to be a valuable property by letting its shares lie round loose for anyone to pick up."

"Ah, you are optimistic, I see. That's because you have been out in the open so much, instead of haunting your father's office."

At this moment the arrival of the automobile was announced, and his lordship rose slowly to his feet.

"I'm going to give you a lift as far as your father's office, and I want you to introduce him to me. I have been looking at this question merely from the mining engineer's standpoint. I should like to know what the city point of view is, and that I shall get from your father, if he is the honest man you say he is. So we will run down into the city together. I suppose the sooner my check is in your bank the better."

"Yes, the bank opens at ten, and it is past that hour now."

"We have taken a little more than our ten minutes," said his lordship, beaming on his guest with that inane smile of his, as they stepped together into the tonneau of a very large red automobile, which was soon humming eastward.

Into the private room of the stockbroker, Mac-keller ushered Lord Stranleigh of Wychwood, and there they found at his desk a rugged-faced, white-haired, haggard-looking man, who glanced up at them with lowering brows.

"I've got five thousand pounds," said the son at once.

"Then run with it to the bank."

"I will, as soon as I have introduced to you Lord Stranleigh of Wychwood. Your lordship will excuse me, I am sure."

"Oh, yes. I stipulated for your absence, you remember, because I do not in the least rely upon your plan," but the young man had departed before his lordship's sentence was finished.

The elder Mackeller looked intently at the newcomer. Being offered a chair, his lordship sat down.

"Is it from you that my son got the money?"

"Yes."

"If you did not believe in his plan, why did you give him the cash?"

"Well, Mr. Mackeller, that is just the question I have been asking myself. I suppose I rather took to him, and in spite of my determination not to, I became interested in the story he told me. I think your seven syndicate men must be rather exceptional, are they not?"

"No. I am exceptional in allowing myself to be caught like a schoolboy."

"I am quite unversed in the ways of the city, Mr. Mackeller, and I should like to know the *modus operandi* of a case like this. Are your seven men personally selling their stock?"

"How do you mean personally? They don't go on the market and trade, of course."

"Then they must employ some one else?"

"Oh, they are employing a score of brokers, all offering the shares with no takers."

"Do you know these brokers, Mr. Mackeller?"

"Every man jack of them."

"Are they enemies of yours?"

"There is neither enmity nor friendship in the city, Lord Stranleigh."

"Your most intimate acquaintance, then, would smash you up all in the way of business?"

"Of course."

"What a den of wild beasts you are!"

"Yes, I have long thought so, and, indeed, with this transaction I had intended to withdraw from the business and settle on my farm. You see, I did not bring up my son—he's the only boy I have—to this business, but unluckily I got nipped just at the moment I intended to stop, as is so often the case. I expected that my holding in this mine would leave me not only well off, but rich, for I have the utmost confidence in my son's report, and my certainty of a fortune caused me to relax my natural caution at exactly the moment when I should have been most wide awake."

"Do you think the five thousand pounds will clear you?"

"I don't know. There's been a panic among those whom I induced to go in with me on this deal, but if I say it myself, my reputation is good, and I think if I can hold on for a week or two longer, the tide will turn. All my life I have endeavored to conduct this business strictly on a truth-telling plan, and that is bound to tell in my favor the moment the panic ceases."

"Do you mean, then, Mr. Mackeller, that the hammering of this mine has caused a financial panic in the city?"

"Oh, no, no! When I refer to a panic, I mean only among those few that have gone in with me; that believed me when I told them this was one of the best things I ever had offered to me. The Red Shallows flotation is too small an affair to cause even a flutter in the city, yet it threatens to grind me to pieces."

"There are, you say, twenty stockbrokers selling these shares, and you know their names. Where do they offer the shares?"

"On the Stock Exchange, in their offices, in the street, anywhere."

"Is there another twenty stockbrokers whom you could trust?"

"Yes."

"Suppose at twelve o'clock to-day, exactly to the minute, your twenty went to the offices of the other twenty, would they find in those offices some one to sell them this stock?"

"Yes."

"Even if the principal were absent?"

"Yes."

"Before selling, would the syndicate score of stockbrokers communicate with each other, or with their principals?"

"I don't know. It would depend on their instructions."

"Suppose they refused to sell when a *bona fide* offer was made?"

"Then the stock would instantly rise, and your five thousand pounds would not be needed. I see what you mean, Lord Stranleigh. You are going to make what they call a bluff. But, you see, they'd instantly unload the stock on you. They wouldn't refuse to sell."

"Ah, I was afraid they would. Very well, Mr. Mackeller, take this commission from me, the first I have ever given in the city. I am more accustomed to gambling in my club, or at Monte Carlo, so I must depend on you to look after the details. Quietly but quickly select your twenty men; give them *carte blanche,* but make it a sure proviso that they each attack the stockbroker you direct them to, at exactly the same moment. Let there be no intercommunication if possible, and tell your twenty to buy everything in sight so far as the Red Shallows are concerned."

"But, my lord, that may take a fortune, and the sellers will insist on immediate payment."

"They will get it, Mr. Mackeller. I am naturally a plunger, and this game fascinates me, because I don't understand it."

"I think you understand it a great deal better than you pretend, my lord, but this may require half a million of money."

"Very well. Get whatever papers ready that are necessary to protect you. I'll place the money at your disposal, and we ought to have all the stock that's for sale by ten minutes after twelve. Your son and I have been doing business on a ten-minutes' basis, but in this case we'll allow half an hour, and see what happens."

The elder Mackeller looked sternly at this dapper young man of the bandbox, so beautiful, so neat, so debonair, so well-groomed, and the young man became so uncomfortable under the fierce scrutiny of those hawklike eyes, that his own drooped modestly like those of a girl, and with the thin, elegant glove which he held loosely in his right hand Stranleigh flicked an invisible particle of dust from his trouser leg.

One need not be deeply versed in human nature to understand the temptation which now assailed the gray-haired stockbroker. It was as if a fawn-colored dove had made an appeal to a bald eagle that had swooped down from its eyrie in the crags where its young lay starving. It was as if a bleating lamb, all alone, were making courteous suggestions to a hungry wolf. Here was reproduced the situation of which city men dream when they enjoy a good night. Here, into the den of a stockbroker had innocently walked a West-end clubman, a titled person, almost shamefully rich, concealing beneath the culture of the colleges an arrogance and an ignorance equally colossal. Here was a fowl to be plucked, and its feathers were not only abundant but of the most costly eiderdown nature, and here the astute Mackeller had the victim entirely to himself, with none to protect or interfere. The aged stockbroker, wise in the ways of the city, and yet but now entrapped by them, drew a long breath and heaved a deep sigh ere he spoke.

"Lord Stranleigh," he said at last, with severity, "it is my duty to warn you that you are putting your foot into a quagmire which may be so bottomless that it will overwhelm you. No man can say what this syndicate has up its sleeve, and once you involve yourself, you may be drawn in and stripped of all your possessions, great as I am told they are. You have given a check for five thousand pounds to my boy, and you say it is because you believed in him. That expression touches my flinty heart. I believe in him, and this belief is about everything of value I retain in the world to-day. Now, if you wish to protect that five thousand, do it by giving him another five, or another. My boy is all I've got left. I'm fighting for him more than for myself. Now here are you, about his own age, yet completely inexperienced in financial trickery, so I cannot allow you to walk blindly into this financial turmoil."

The young man looked up at the speaker, and his smile was singularly winning. The usual vacant expression of his countenance had given place to pleasurable animation.

"But you are experienced, Mr. Mackeller?"

"Yes, and see where my experience has landed me. I'm up to the neck, yes, to the very lips, in this foul quagmire; a bankrupt at a word from my banker."

"Are you a college man, Mr. Mackeller?"

"No."

"Perhaps you have little faith in a college training?"

"I have none at all for a practical man. It is the worst training in the world for a person who is to be engaged in business."

"In that case, Mr. Mackeller, I hesitate to cite a historical instance which occurred to my mind when your son was talking to me of your syndicate of seven. As the incident is six hundred years old, it is unlikely to impress a modern city man. Nevertheless, there was once upon this earth a syndicate of seven much more powerful and important than your johnnies. The chief of this syndicate was Jaques de Molay, Grand Master of the Templars, and the other six were his powerful, pious officers. They were arrogant people, and their wealth was enormous. Kings and noblemen had deposited their treasures with the Templars, the bankers of that time, and the Order was so rich it had become a menace to the world. Why, your seven nonentities, with which you try to frighten me, are mere helpless puppets compared with those seven giants of finance, and besides money this notable seven had an armed force of veterans at their back before whom even a king with his army might tremble. But Philippe le Bel, King of France, did not tremble. He worked in on the seven the twelve-o'clock rule that I am recommending to you. At high noon, on the 13th October, 1307 (please note the fatal conjunction of the two thirteens) every Templar in France was arrested. He gave them no chance of communicating with each other. The army of the Templars lay helpless and officerless. The wealth of the Templars was at the mercy of the king. The syndicated seven were burned at the stake in Paris.

"I imagine that your son thought my attention wandered two or three times during his narrative. I saw him set his jaw as one who says 'I will interest this man in spite of his brainlessness.' But I was thinking of the magnificent simultaneousness of the king's action, and I have no doubt the Mackeller of his day warned him of his danger in meddling with the Templars. An unholy desire filled me to try this six-century-old method, the king's move, as we would say at chess, on our modern and alert city. I have some loose cash in the bank, and don't need to sell any securities. For the last ten years my income has been thirty thousand pounds annually, and very seldom have I spent more than five thousand of that sum in one twelvemonth. My automobile is at your door, and at your disposal. You and I will drive first to my bankers, and arrange that there will be no hitch so far as cash is concerned; then I shall take a cab to my club. Telephone number, 15760 Mayfair. Just note that down, please. Now what are the shares of Red Shallows selling for this morning?"

"They opened at two shillings and sevenpence on the pound share, but have dropped several points since."

"Ah, well, a few hundred thousand pounds will buy quite a quantity of half-crown shares, and if we act simultaneously, as the king struck, we will acquire everything in sight before the stuff has time to rise. Come along, Mr. Mackeller, there's not a moment to lose. If you organize this sortie in silence and effectively, you will show the savage seven there's life in the old dog yet."

At ten minutes after one that day a large red automobile drew up in front of the Camperdown Club on Pall Mall, and Mackeller with his son stepped out of it. Lord Stranleigh met them in the hall apparently cool and unexcited, but he was coming away from the tape machine, which was recording that Red Shallows were leaping up toward par. Lord Stranleigh led his visitors in to the Strangers' Room, which was empty, and closed the door.

"Well, my lord," said Mackeller, "those fools have sold some fifty thousand shares more of stock than there is in existence."

"It seems to me," drawled his lordship, "although I know nothing of city ways, that such overselling is injudicious."

"Injudicious!" shouted young Mackeller, "why, you've got them like that," and he raised his huge fist into the air and clenched it with a force resembling hydraulic pressure. "You can smash them. They can't deliver. They've not only lost the mine, but you can ruin them by placing any price you please on the shares they've sold and cannot produce."

"That's true," corroborated old Mackeller, nodding his head, "and the bank didn't use your five-thousand-pound check after all."

"Here it is," said the young man, producing it.

"Ah, well," said Lord Stranleigh, slipping the paper into his waistcoat pocket. "Let us be thankful you two are just in time to join me at an excellent meal. I've been expecting you, and I've ordered a French lunch in honor of the late Philippe le Bel. He burned his syndicate of seven at the stake, but we'll merely burn our syndicate's fingers."

CHAPTER II—THE PREMATURE COMPROMISE

THE Camperdown Club in Pall Mall is famous for its cuisine, and young Lord Stranleigh of Wychwood provided a lunch on the day of the great coup that was notable even in the Camperdown. The elder Mackeller did justice to the prime vintage which his lordship shared with him, but young Mackeller proved to be a water drinker. After lunch they retired to a small private smoking room, where they could review the situation without being interrupted, and here coffee, liquors, cigars, and cigarettes were set out, and the waiter retired.

"It would seem, then," began his lordship, "that you and I, Mr. Mackeller, are owners of a property situated somewhere along the west coast of Africa, a dozen miles or so up a river whose name I do not remember, and which I could not pronounce if I did."

"The Paramakaboo," interjected Mackeller, junior.

"Thanks," drawled Lord Stranleigh. "The property is known as the Red Shallows: I suppose because gold is red and the deposit is on the surface."

The two Mackellers nodded.

"I hope I am not unduly confident when I take it for granted that there are no 'buses running to Para-what-you-call-it, nor steam launches either?"

"No," said Peter Mackeller, "it is several hundred miles from the nearest port of call by any of the regular liners, or even tramp steamers. Once there, you must charter whatever kind of sailing craft is available, for the mouth of the Paramakaboo."

"I see. Now, I presume, Mr. Mackeller, that, being an adept at this sort of thing, you have made your purchases of shares strictly according to the rules of the game. No hole is left for this syndicate of seven to crawl out, is there?"

"No," said the elder Mackeller.

"They will probably try to wriggle away," suggested Stranleigh, "as soon as they learn they are trapped."

"Undoubtedly," replied Angus Mackeller, "but I see no way of escape except through the court of bankruptcy, which is a road these men won't want to travel, and even if they did, they have lost all this property, at any rate. They've done themselves out of Red Shallows, whatever happens."

"How many shares did you buy, Mr. Mackeller?"

"In round numbers, three hundred thousand."

"And how much did that cost me?"

"Again in round numbers, thirty-seven thousand, five hundred pounds. Some of the stock was bought as low as two-and-four, the bulk at half a crown, and a quantity of shares at two-and-seven and two-and-eight. I'm reckoning the lot to average half a crown a share."

"How many shares does the company possess?"

"The authorized capital of the company is £250,000 in shares of one pound each. Fifty thousand shares were sold to provide working capital, and ten thousand allotted to me for forming the company, and securing the fifty thousand pounds without publicity."

"Well, Mr. Mackeller, my head is useless so far as figures are concerned, but it seems to me, speaking heedlessly, that these men have promised to deliver to me sixty thousand shares, the bulk of which does not exist, while the rest is in our possession."

"More than that, Lord Stranleigh," replied Mackeller, "because I bought a quantity of shares in addition to the ten thousand allotted me; then three or four of my colleagues have not sold, including your friend, the Honorable John Hazel."

"Well, then, it would appear that these syndicate johnnies have bitten off more than they can chew, as they say out West. How soon will they discover the particulars of the situation?"

"They doubtless know it now, my lord."

"And what will be their first move?"

"They will probably endeavor to compromise."

"Which means they will try to see you, for of course they know nothing of me in this transaction."

"It is very likely they will approach me."

"What will you do, Mr. Mackeller?"

"I shall await your instructions."

"Oh, my instructions are of no value. I'm a mere amateur, you know, whose dependence is on you. What is your advice, Mr. Mackeller?"

"I should compromise if I were you."

"Yes, an Englishman dearly loves a compromise, doesn't he? But if I thought these fellows would put up a decent and interesting fight, I should like to see them squirm."

"That isn't business, my lord."

"Isn't it? Well, what would the city call business in this instance?"

"Strip them of everything they possess, short of making them bankrupt."

"Oh, that's a beastly sort of compromise! That's the city's idea of fair play, is it? Well, I'm blest! They'd surely fight if confronted with such a prospect as that."

"How can they fight? They've undertaken to turn over to you anywhere from sixty to seventy thousand shares of Red Shallows, which they do not possess, and cannot obtain. You're the only man in the world from whom they can buy this material which they have sold. There is no competition in this deal. They must pay the price you ask. If you say these shares you bought for two-and-sixpence are now worth ten pounds, they must pay the difference, or go broke."

"Well, Mr. Mackeller, that seems simple enough, doesn't it? The only information I need is how much money these fellows possess. How shall I set about finding out?"

"Your bank could give you a pretty close estimate, and I'll inquire at mine."

"Then that's all settled. I'm cast for the hardhearted villain in the piece, I suppose?"

"Yes, you may be hard-hearted or the reverse, just which you choose."

"Will their women and children come and plead with me, on their knees, with tears in their eyes?"

"I've known that done, my lord, but I've never heard that it has had any effect in the city."

"I think I'll turn that job over to you, Mr. Mac-keller. You'll be my plea-receiver. I dislike having my emotions worked upon. They tell me that a harrowing of the emotions causes wrinkles and sallowness, and I'm particularly careful of my complexion. Both you and your son seem to have neglected these simple precautions, for your complexions are irretrievably ruined; yours through leading a hard-hearted life in the city, and his by yachting on the river Paraboola."

"Paramakaboo," corrected young Mackeller.

"Thanks, so it is. How should we make the first move toward gathering in those shares which do not exist?"

"I suggest," replied the elder man, "that you should formally demand that the president of the company and the board of directors turn over to you all the papers and belongings of the company, also its balance at the bank, also the resignations of the president and each of the directors. Give them legal notice that no check is to be drawn upon the bank account."

"How much money do you suppose is left in the bank?"

The younger man answered.

"They have chartered the tramp steamer Rajah, which now lies at Southampton. I was in charge of its fitting out. A few thousand pounds have been spent in surface-mining machinery, in provisions, and in corrugated iron for the building of shelters for the engineering staff and workmen. It was not the intention at first to erect a smelting furnace at the mine, but to load the ship with ore, and send her back to England. I returned to London from Southampton, when my father telegraphed to me about the crisis in the affairs of the company. I had spent less than five thousand pounds, so there should be forty or forty-five thousand pounds in the bank."

"I suppose," suggested his lordship, in a tone of supreme indifference, "that they have probably drawn the whole amount out by this time, and perhaps have divided it among the immaculate seven."

"In that case," replied the elder, "they will be forced to account for every penny of it."

The conference was here interrupted by a gentle knock at the door, and one of the club servants, entering, presented a card to Lord Stran-leigh, which bore the words, "Jacob Hahn; Hahn and Lewishon, Solicitors, Frankfort Buildings, Bucklersbury."

"I don't know this man," said his lordship, looking at the servant. "Are you sure he asked for me?"

"Yes, my lord."

"Perhaps it's you he wishes to see, Mr. Mac-keller. Do you know Jacob Hahn, solicitor?"

"Oh, yes, Hahn and Lewishon. They are solicitors for the syndicate, and also solicitors for your Red Shallows company."

"Ah, quite so! Had I better see him, or shall I refer him to you at your office?"

"As this is a private room, my lord, and as there are three of us present, while he will be alone, I think it would do no harm to hear what he has to say."

"Very good. Bring him in."

Jacob Hahn proved to be a big, genial-looking man, with a cast of countenance that gave but a very slight hint of Hebraic origin. Despite the air of confidence with which he advanced, he seemed to be somewhat taken aback at seeing Mackeller and his son seated there. He nodded to them with a smile of good fellowship, nevertheless, and said to the elder man:

"Perhaps, Mr. Mackeller, you will introduce me to Lord Stranleigh of Wychwood."

"That is as his lordship says," commented Mackeller grimly, but Lord Stranleigh rose to his feet with a smile as engaging as that of the solicitor.

"I think no introduction is necessary, Mr. Hahn, for I understand you and your partner represent me, temporarily, at least, so far as the Red Shallows property is concerned. Pray, take a chair, Mr. Hahn. May I offer you some coffee, and what liquor do you prefer?"

"No liquor, if your lordship pleases. Thanks for the coffee."

"Then help yourself, Mr. Hahn, to cigars and cigarettes, whichever you prefer. You'll find them not half bad."

"Thank you."

"How did you know I was interested in the gold mine, Mr. Hahn?"

"Ah, your lordship, it is our business to make these little discoveries. I called at Mackeller's office, but no one knew where he was. I realized, however, that he had not been the financier of this rather startling incursion, and it was not long before I learned the facts of the matter. Oh, not at your office, Mr. Mackeller! There was no one there but that most discreet old man who is even more difficult to pump than you are yourself. I've tried it with both of you on various occasions, so I am quite competent to make a comparison," and with this, the good-natured man laughed. "I then drove to your residence, my lord, and finally to this club, on the chance of finding you."

"Ah, you city chaps are so clever, Mr. Hahn, that it is easy for you to catch us less alert people of the West End."

The solicitor laughed heartily, as if he greatly admired Lord Stranleigh's remark. He was a very friendly person, and beamed upon the young nobleman in a most ingratiating manner.

"I'm afraid it's the other way about, my lord. I happen to know several stockbrokers who within the past few hours have come to the conclusion that the West End is up to snuff, as one might say. There are some people in the city who have been caught, to repeat your own word."

"Really? Have some of the stockbrokers been getting nipped? I always understood they were a very sharp body of men."

"They are generally supposed to be, my lord, but in the case we were just speaking of, some of them tell me they have oversold; that is to say, they have promised to deliver shares which are not at present in their possession, a rather reckless thing to do."

"Oh! then it was the stockbrokers who made that mistake, was it?"

"Yes, some of them exceeded their instructions. They knew that there were in existence some two hundred and fifty thousand shares, and when our shrewd friend here, Mr. Mackeller, approached them for five or ten thousand, some of them imagining they could get practically as many more as they desired—for the stock had been kicking about London for a week with no takers, and, being temporarily blinded by the commission they were to receive, and the fact that the purchase was a cash transaction, which I imagine they had some doubt of Mr. Mackeller's ability to make good—they pressed upon him more shares than had been given them to sell, and now they are in rather a panic. I think I am correct in saying, Mr. Mackeller, that in several instances you were offered more shares than you asked for?"

"I didn't ask for shares at all," gruffly responded Mackeller, "but I learn from my brokers that in all instances they were offered more shares than they required, but my instructions were definite enough, which were to accept and pay for all the shares they could get. In one or two cases, my brokers telephoned to me for instructions, and I suppose that's how the news got out that they were acting for me, and if these brokers of yours thought they were pushing farther into a corner a man already there, they can't expect much sympathy from me when they find themselves in the corner instead."

"Ah, no one would be optimistic enough to expect sympathy from *you*, Mr. Mackeller," pursued the lawyer.

"Then they won't be disappointed when they don't get it," curtly commented Mackeller.

"I beg your pardon, Mr. Hahn," interposed Stranleigh, "but am I to take it you have come to see me on behalf of these unfortunate stockbrokers?"

"No, my lord. I represent Mr. Conrad Schwartzbrod and his colleagues."

"Oh! and who is Mr. Schwartzbrod?"

Before the solicitor could reply, Mackeller said, with lowering brows:

"He is the head of the syndicate, the president of your company, and his colleagues are the board of directors."

"I see, I see. Then Mr. Schwartzbrod and his friends are not sufferers by this little deal of mine?"

"Oh! bless you, no, Lord Stranleigh, except in so far as they have parted with their property a little more cheaply than they had intended. I believe Mr. Schwartzbrod considers that a fair price for the shares would have been from three-and-six to four shillings."

"I'm not very good at figures," complained his lordship, with a slight wrinkle in his forehead, "but if three-and-six is a fair price, then the loss of the syndicate is merely a shilling a share, and as they sold me three hundred thousand shares, that comes to—" He looked helplessly at Mac-keller.

"Fifteen thousand pounds," said Mackeller sharply.

"Ah, thanks. Fifteen thousand pounds. Well, that divided between seven amounts to——"

Again he turned an appealing eye to the somber Mackeller, who replied promptly:

"Two thousand one hundred and forty-two pounds, six shillings each."

"I'm ever so much obliged, Mackeller. What a deuce of an advantage it is to possess brains! I am told that east of the Danube people cannot figure up simple little sums in their mind, and so this gives the Jews a great advantage over them in commercial dealings, which adds to the wealth of the Jew, but detracts from his popularity. I fear the inability to count often begins west of Regent Street, and afflicts many of us who are accustomed to paying the waiter at the club exactly what he demands. But to return to our muttons, Mr. Hahn, I must congratulate you on the fact that your clients, who I understand are rich and estimable men, lose merely a couple of thousand each on a deal involving some hundreds of thousands, although it occupied but a few minutes of the time of forty stockbrokers acting simultaneously. I suppose as the amount of their loss is so trifling, you have not come here to make any appeal for clemency on behalf of the respectable Mr. Schwartzbrod and his colleagues?"

"Oh, not at all, your lordship. No, Mr. Schwartzbrod is merely anxious that the transfer should be made in such a way as to give you as little trouble as possible."

"I'm delighted to hear you say that, Mr. Hahn, because the sole purpose of my life is to avoid trouble. I employ no less than twelve solicitors to intercept whatever trouble comes to hand so that it doesn't get past them to me. I should be glad to take on another solicitor, but that would make thirteen, which is a very unlucky number, Mr. Hahn. Mr. Schwartzbrod and his partners, then, will put no difficulties in my way?"

"Oh, none in the least, Lord Stranleigh. They have commissioned me to convey their compliments and congratulations to your lordship on the acquirement of what they consider a very valuable property."

"Oh, not so valuable, Mr. Hahn. Only a shilling a share, you know. Still, I believe that's considered a reasonably profitable margin. I don't know exactly what per cent it runs to, but——"

"Forty per cent," snapped Mackeller.

"Is it really? Well, I think I'm only getting four on a large portion of my money. I must speak to my investment solicitor about this. If a mere amateur like myself can make forty per cent in ten minutes, don't you think a solicitor should do better than content himself with four per cent in a whole year?"

"Your investment solicitor probably takes no risk, Lord Stranleigh."

"Ah, that will be it. I knew there was a flea on the wall somewhere, but, you see, I'm not well versed in these things. But I interrupted you, Mr. Hahn. You were going to say——"

"I was going to say, my lord, that there are two hundred and fifty thousand shares in the company, all of which are now vested in yourself, Mr. Mackeller, and probably one or two others. Of course the unfortunate stockbrokers cannot produce the fifty thousand shares or more that are not in existence, and I don't suppose your lordship has any thought of forcing these people into bankruptcy merely because of a little overzealousness on their part. *Noblesse oblige*, you know."

"Ah, quite so. *Noblesse oblige*. I thought the phrase hadn't penetrated yet into the city." Again the solicitor laughed heartily.

"A fair hit. A fair hit, my lord. Well, as I was about to add, Mr. Schwartzbrod and his friends are prepared to transfer to you instantly this property if you desire this to be done."

"Yes, I rather think that is my desire. You see, when a man buys a thing, and pays the money for it, he usually expects it to be turned over, don't you know?"

"Quite so, my lord. I have brought with me the documents pertaining to the transfer, all duly made out, signed and sealed, ready for delivery. But it occurred to my principals that perhaps you did not care yourself to develop the property, and perhaps your intention was to take what you considered a fair profit on the transaction, and relinquish whatever claim you possess on this land. You would thus make a clear gain, and run no further risk."

"Mining is a somewhat uncertain business, isn't it, Mr. Hahn?"

"Personally, I have had no experience with it, my lord, but they tell me that gold-mining is about the most hazardous occupation that a man can adopt. If he is not a practical miner, he is swindled on all hands by those to whom he intrusts the operations."

"I'm afraid I am not a practical man, Mr. Hahn, and know as little about gold-mining as you do."

"In that ease, Lord Stranleigh, I think we should have no difficulty in arriving at an understanding acceptable to both sides."

"I should be delighted. What do your principals consider a fair profit?"

"That is a matter for mutual discussion, my lord. They propose to pay you back the amount you have invested, and in addition to that hand over to you, say fifteen or twenty thousand pounds. Or they would be willing that you should retain a substantial holding in the venture if you wish to profit by their experience, and that there should be a *pro rata* deduction from the amount they are to hand over to you."

"I see. Well, that is very good of them, but as I told Mr. Maekeller to-day, I am by way of being a plunger. It is all or nothing with me, and so, having in a manner of speaking been drawn into the vortex, I think I'll stay in and see what happens. That being the case, I think it would be most unfair to make others share a risk over which they could exercise no control. I dare say I am very stupid. My friend, Jack Hazel, who knows city men and their ways, says that it is a practice there to minimize risk by spreading it over a number of persons, but I shouldn't be happy, if my plans went wrong, to think that others were suffering through my foolishness. I should feel toward them as Mr. Schwartzbrod feels toward those unfortunate stockbrokers who exceeded his instructions, a sentiment which does him great credit. So, if you don't mind, I think we will confine our attention to the simple transfer you propose."

"Very good, my lord. Whatever plan commends itself the more strongly to your lordship will be cheerfully acquiesced in by my principals. Here, then, are the papers which make over the gold fields to you, and if you will just sign this formal receipt we may regard the transaction as complete."

"My dear Mr. Hahn, it is a pleasure to deal with a man of your courtesy and comprehension."

His lordship, with a bow, took up the papers the other had laid down on the table, glanced at them, and passed them along to Angus Mackeller, who scrutinized them with the eye of a hawk. His lordship then read very slowly the document he had been asked to sign, and he took a long time in his examination, during which period the keen eyes of the solicitor could scarcely conceal their apprehension. At last his lordship laid it down.

"I am somewhat at a disadvantage," he said, "among legal instruments. As I informed you, I am fortunate in possessing the services of a dozen sharper men than myself who are good enough, for a consideration, to advise me on these topics. But, alas! not one of them is present at this moment."

"Why, my lord, I don't think you have any reason to complain. I'm here alone, without any corroborative witness on my behalf, while there are three of you sitting here."

"Ah, now you speak, Mr. Hahn, as if we were contestants—combatants, as one might say—instead of being a quartette of friends. There is no need of witnesses where everything has gone on as smoothly as has been the case since you entered this room. You represent men who are only too anxious to do the right thing, and you meet, I hope, a man who is desirous of effecting a compromise, and I think I may say the same for my friend Mackeller. I am sure nothing would give Mackeller greater pleasure than to treat Mr. Schwartzbrod in the same generous, equitable way in which Mr. Schwartzbrod would treat him." The solicitor leaned back in his chair, while his smile became a sort of fixed grin.

"Precisely, precisely," he murmured.

"Of course I don't pretend to penetrate into all the intricacies of this apparently simple little receipt, but it seems to me that in Mr. Schwartzbrod's generous desire to protect his stockbrokers, he is doing so, doubtless unconsciously, at my expense."

"At your expense, my lord?"

"Well, that's the way it looks to me. These stockbrokers, poor devils, must produce some sixty or seventy thousand shares on which they cannot lay their hands, and this, as my ancient friend Euclid used to remark, is impossible. Now, if I sign this receipt, it appears that I waive all claim against these unfortunate, but nevertheless careless stockbrokers."

"I thought it was understood, my lord, that, as you obtained quiet possession of the gold field, you were not inclined to push to the wall—I think that is your own phrase—a number of men who, as things are going in the city this year, have not been overburdened with business. Indeed, the stagnation in financial circles, the high bank rate, and all that, doubtless accounts for the eagerness with which these men, regarding the honest commission they were earning, ventured to overstep the bounds set for them, thus placing themselves, as one may say, at your mercy. I somehow took it for granted that you had no animus against this unlucky score."

"Animus? Oh, no, bless my soul, not the least. Animus is an emotion I confess I scarcely know the meaning of. I think all my friends will tell you I am a most good-natured chap, who would rather forgive an injury than remember it."

"I am delighted to hear you say so, my lord, and admit that, for the moment, I was slightly apprehensive."

"Your apprehensions were quite groundless, Mr. Hahn; quite groundless, I assure you. I shall not injure one of your stockbrokers, and when you report my words to the kindly Mr. Schwartzbrod and his colleagues, I can fancy with what relief they will hear your repetition of them."

"Thank you, my lord, I shall have great pleasure in telling them what you have said."

"On the other hand, Mr. Hahn, justice is justice, as you yourself would be the first to admit. I am entitled to what Mr. Schwartzbrod and his coadjutors would call fair profit on these sixty or seventy thousand shares they cannot produce. Now, although I am so ignorant of business methods, I nevertheless believe that a principal is responsible for the actions of his agents. My chauffeur was fined, down in Surrey the other day, for exceeding the speed limit. I was not in the car, but here in my club. Nevertheless, I was compelled to pay the fine and the costs, because the chauffeur was in my employ. The syndicate of seven, animated, as I believe, by a desire to crush Mr. Mackeller and possess themselves, not only of all his stock, but of the shares of his friends who paid a pound each for them, forgot during one critical ten minutes that a buyer might happen along who had some money in his pockets. It is due to the energy and the persuasive powers of this young engineer here, formerly in their employ, that a purchaser materialized at the crucial moment. I think it is a fact that if Mr. Schwartz-brod and his distinguished company of pirates had not jauntily run up the black flag with the skull and crossbones on it, they would not be today in the place of jeopardy in which they stand. To continue my nautical simile, they thought Mr. Mackeller here was an unprotected merchantman, and proceeded to board and scuttle him, when over the horizon there appeared the latest thing in turbine twenty-five-knot-an-hour cruisers, armed with 4.7 guns, or whatever bally pieces of artillery such a cruiser carries. Now, after presenting the good Mr. Schwartzbrod with my compliments, tell him not to lose any sleep because of the unfortunate stockbrokers, because I am going to attack him, not them. If, in the scrimmage, any of the stockbrokers go under, I will set them up in business again, but I shall not do so at my own expense. I shall simply raise my price to the immaculate syndicate of seven."

All geniality had departed from the solicitor's face, leaving it hard as granite.

"I think you are threatening us, Lord Stran-leigh," he said.

"Oh, dear me, no. How can you put such a construction on my words? I am merely making a suggestion. You will leave with me all those transfer papers. You will ask Schwartzbrod and the six directors to send me their resignations. You will warn them not to draw a penny from the bank account of the company."

"The bank account of the company is already overdrawn," said the solicitor; then apparently thinking he had spoken a little prematurely, added hastily: "at least, so I understand. They have gone in largely for materials necessary for the development of the property."

"Oh, that is very interesting, Mr. Hahn. You don't happen to know at what time to-day the money was taken out?"

"I didn't say it was taken out to-day. I don't know when it was withdrawn."

"Of course not. Still, that is a trifle that really doesn't matter, and doubtless your principals will ask of me to allow them quietly to replace it."

"I cannot leave these transfer papers with you unless you sign that receipt. You know enough of business to understand that, I suppose. A man like myself, acting merely as agent, must have documentary proof that he has fulfilled his duty. If I leave the papers with you, I must bear away the signed receipt in lieu of them."

"I'll willingly sign a receipt, Mr. Hahn, simply acknowledging your delivery of the papers."

"My instructions were quite definite, my lord, and I dare not vary from them."

"Oh, I thought that Mr. Schwartzbrod had placed negotiations entirely in your hands, and would do as you advised."

"I shall, of course, give him my best advice, but I honestly could not advise him to part with all his advantages in the situation, and receive nothing in return."

"His advantages? What are they?"

"Well, my lord, they are probably greater than you imagine. He and his colleagues have been elected president and board of directors of the Red Shallows company. They hold office for a year. You spoke just now of the withdrawal of the money. It is quite within their legal right to not only withdraw the money, but to issue debentures against the shares that you hold. If you read the articles of association, you will see that this is so. Although you hold all the shares of the company, you cannot compel them to resign, and you cannot vote your stock until the next annual meeting, which is nearly twelve months distant. During that time the president and board of directors, who are clothed with large powers, for I myself drew up the articles of association, and I know their contents—these seven men may do practically what they please with your property, unless we come to an amicable settlement."

"Ah, who is threatening now, Mr. Hahn?"

"I am not, my lord. I am merely telling you, in the plainest possible words at my command, just how the situation stands."

"I thank you, Mr. Hahn, for the clarity of your explanation. I take it, then, that you cannot leave these documents with me?"

"Not unless you will sign that receipt, my lord."

"As I feel disinclined to do that, Mr. Hahn, and suffer no qualms of conscience whatever regarding the unlucky stockbrokers, I hereby return them to you, receipt and all. Now, you tell Mr. Schwartzbrod that the price of Red Shallows shares is one hundred pounds each, and if there are seventy thousand shares coming to me which your principles cannot produce, their check for seven million pounds will do me quite as well."

"My lord, you pretend ignorance in business affairs. I suppose you are now trying to prove it. You cannot make the shares a hundred pounds apiece, nor can you enforce such an exorbitant condition through any court in the land. My principals would receive relief from any court of equity."

"It is not my intention, Mr. Hahn, to trouble the courts with the matter at all. In fact, I refuse to accept cash from your principals. They have sold me the shares, and I insist on the delivery of those shares. I happen to be the only person in the world who owns the shares, and my price for each share is a hundred pounds. Your principals will be compelled to beg me to sell them the shares. As a matter of fact, I do not intend to place any such figure upon them. I merely used a hundred pounds as an illustration. Of course, if I put them at that price I would break your principals, and no court in the kingdom could save them. To be perfectly frank with you, for I do not possess the mental qualification necessary to cope with business men of genius such as I doubt not your principals are, I will now tell you what I intend to do. I shall put the price of shares at exactly what your people sold them to the public for, that is, one pound each. They cannot complain of my doing what they have done themselves, now can they? It is true that I bought these shares at two-and-six, but that also was not my fault. They, by throwing their shares on the market, knocked down the price to the figure I have named, and I bought the shares from the stockbrokers of your principals. If you say their action was not done to embarrass Mr. Mac-keller, then I at once accept your statement as true. For some other reason they battered down the price from one pound to half a crown. A few weeks ago they had sold fifty thousand of these shares for one pound each, and because of their unexplained smashing of the market, these good people lost a large portion of the money they had paid out. Now surely, surely, being a just and equitable man, your Mr. Schwartzbrod cannot refuse to drink the cup he has himself brewed. He could not show even the court of equity that I was doing a usurious thing in placing the stock back at the figure he himself originally settled, in following the illustrious example of Mr. Schwartzbrod himself. Now, I leave it to you, Mr. Hahn, as a fair and just man, whose indignant expostulation at my figure of a hundred pounds was most laudable, and entirely to your credit, are you not surprised at my moderation?"

"I should hardly go so far as to say that, my lord. This stock cost you thirty thousand pounds."

"Oh, don't underestimate, Mr. Hahn, it cost thirty-seven thousand five hundred pounds."

"Even in that case you are asking my principals to pay double. In other words, you will have deprived them of their property, getting it not only for nothing, but with a bonus of thirty odd thousand pounds in cash. If that is not an act of piracy, as you said, what in the name of Heaven is?"

His lordship shrugged his shoulders, and spread forth his hands. His expression showed that he was grieved and disappointed.

"Then instead of thanking me— —"

He sighed deeply and did not continue the sentence.

"As I have informed you, Lord Stranleigh, my principals are not liable to you for those seventy thousand shares. You must seek your remedy against the stockbrokers."

"That is exactly what I shall not do."

"Then you will be non-suited in the courts."

"But, my dear sir, haven't I been telling you I'm not going to the courts? Like all respectable pirates, I abominate a court of law. It's such a waste of time, don't you know. Not only shall I take no action against the stockbrokers, but if your principals do not agree in writing also to take no action against them the price of shares shall rise suddenly. I am so much in sympathy with Mr. Schwartzbrod's tender feelings toward the stockbrokers that I intend to protect them, and I am sure you will forgive me if I say that I very much doubt if any of the stockbrokers exceeded their instructions, even though times are hard in the city."

"Then," said Mr. Hahn, rising, and replacing the documents he brought once more in his inside pocket, "that is your ultimatum, is it?"

"I beg you, Mr. Hahn, not to give to my poor and stammering remarks so harsh a term. Ultimatum? Bless us all, no. I'm no President Kruger, but merely a somewhat lackadaisical man who is innocent of many of the ways of this wicked world. I hope you won't represent me to the virtuous Mr. Schwartzbrod as a hard, contentious fellow. Tell him that I'm the most easy person in the world to deal with. Tell him the moment he sends me his check for seventy thousand pounds—I hope it will be a little less—Mr. Mackeller here will figure out the exact amount, and run it into shillings and pence, and even farthings if necessary—the moment I get that check, the resignations, the guarantee that no harm will be done to the simple-minded stockbrokers, the balance in the bank, and some account of everything the company has done since it came into existence until the time it fell into my hands, why, tell him he has no greater admirer or well-wisher than myself."

"I shall give him your message, my lord."

"Do, but add to it that charming Biblical text, 'Agree with thine adversary quickly.' I think there's something about squaring up things before the sun goes down, but I shan't be so hasty as all that. Stock will remain at a pound during tomorrow. Next day it will rise a shilling, next day another shilling, the third day a third shilling. It's so very easy to keep count of; just make a red mark on your calendar to-day, and if he allows two weeks to go past, why, there's fourteen shillings added to the twenty he would have had to pay before."

The solicitor, who would have made an excellent actor, forced a laugh that did not sound half bad.

"Ah, you are joking now, my lord."

"I don't think so, Mr. Hahn, although I do sometimes joke unconsciously."

"You will, I am sure, give us a week to think this matter over."

"Oh, very well. Anything for the sake of peace and quietness, and an amicable settlement. I should hate Mr. Schwartzbrod to think me exacting. Now, don't go away thinking I'm reluctant to make concessions, and big ones. That's seven shillings a share I am giving you, and on seventy thousand shares—how much is that, Mr. Mackeller, you know I've no head for figures?"

"Twenty-four thousand five hundred pounds."

"Why, look at that, Mr. Hahn. Here are you, who refuse to leave me those documents you carry, who have been thinking hard of me—there, don't deny it; I saw it by the expression of your countenance—here am I giving to Mr. Schwartz-brod and the delectable six a present of—of—of——"

"Twenty-four thousand five hundred pounds," prompted Mackeller the elder.

"Yes, twenty-four thousand five hundred pounds in hard cash, bestowing it upon men I never saw, and up till to-day never even heard of. I don't want to boast of my virtues, Mr. Hahn, but I doubt if you could find any man in the city who would so jauntily fling away twenty-four thousand five hundred pounds. I got the amount correct that time, Mackeller. I'm improving, you see."

"Very good, my lord. Shall I communicate with you further at this club?"

"No. Hereafter our interviews must be on a hard business basis. The generous nature of our '78 wine makes me a little open-handed. The next interview will take place at Mr. Mackeller's office in the city any time that suits your convenience, and I should be glad to have twenty-four hours' notice, because I mustn't devote my whole life to finance, don't you know, for I am rather fond of automobiling, and may be out of town."

"Thank you. Good afternoon, my lord. Good afternoon, Mr. Mackeller."

The solicitor departed, and Lord Stranleigh smiled at his two companions, who had sat so long silent.

"Well, my young chap," said the frowning Mackeller, drawing a deep breath, "if you ever get to understand finance, God help the city!" His lordship indulged in a laugh, then turned to Peter and said:

"I think you should resume your place at Southampton. You were seeing to the loading of a ship—what did you call it?"

"The *Rajah*—the steamer *Rajah*."

"Well, even if I am not president or board of directors, I ask you to resume that occupation. You are still officially engineer for the company, I take it?"

"Yes."

"Very good. Say not a word to anybody, but go down to Southampton, and proceed with getting the machinery and provisions into the steamer, just as if nothing had happened. If you meet any opposition, telegraph me, and I think I can overcome the obstruction."

So Peter took himself off to Southampton, and met with no obstacle in resuming his duties.

The syndicate consumed the full week, and made an appointment with Mr. Mackeller and Lord Stranleigh on the last day before the shares would begin to go up. This time Mr. Hahn did not appear, but Conrad Schwartzbrod, unmistakably German and unmistakably Hebraic, came cringing in. He spent hours trying to get improved terms, and indeed Lord Stranleigh made him several important concessions. At last he delivered over everything that was demanded, and got from Lord Stranleigh a signed document giving Conrad Schwartzbrod full acquittance of everything he had done up to date. This document was witnessed by Mackeller, and, placing it safely in his pocketbook, the old financier cringed out of the office with an evil leer that would have done credit to the late Sir Henry Irving's *Shy-lock*.

"I wouldn't have conceded an inch to him," said the stern Mackeller.

"Ah, well, what does it matter. If he'd treated a little longer I'd have given him easier terms yet, so I'm glad he's gone."

A telegraph messenger entered the room with a dispatch for Mr. Mackeller, who tore it open, read it, and swore. It was from his son.

"Do not settle with those scoundrels," it ran. "Three days ago when I was seeing to the storing of cargo in the Rajah, I was battened down in the hold, and the steamer sailed. I was put ashore with the pilot, and have just been landed at Plymouth."

"By God!" cried Mackeller, bringing his fist down on the desk. "That document you have signed and I have witnessed, gives him quittance for this theft of the steamer. Now they are going to loot the surface gold and recoup themselves. They have three days' start of us, and it will take a week to get a steamer and fit her out."

His lordship's countenance was serene, and he blew slowly some rings of cigarette smoke up into the air.

"I can't help admiring the courage of old Schwartzbrod," he said. "Think how fine he cut it! And yet it might disturb him to know I'm a friend of the Honorable Mr. Parsons."

"What has that to do with it?" growled Mackeller.

"Nothing, except that the speed of the *Rajah* is seven knots an hour, and my large yacht, *The Woman in White*, lying in Plymouth Harbor, is fitted with Parsons's latest turbines and can, at a pinch, steam twenty-five knots an hour. Poor old Schwartzbrod! We're going to have some fun with him after all."

CHAPTER III—THE MISSION OF "THE WOMAN IN WHITE"

THE breakfast room of Lord Stranleigh's town house was a most cheerful apartment, and the young man who entered sat down to a repast which was at once abundant and choice. The appointments could scarcely have been bettered; the spotless linen, the polished silver, the prismatic cut glass, and the dainty porcelain, formed a pleasant table picture, enhanced by the pile of luscious fruit, the little rolls of cool, golden butter, the crisp white crescents, the brown toast, while the aroma of celestial coffee from the silver urn over a small electric furnace was enough to spur the longing of a sybarite. It is perhaps to be regretted that truth compels record of the fact that the languid person who found himself confronted by delicacies in season and out was healthily hungry, for some of us grumble that to him that hath shall be given, which seems unfair, and there appears to be a human satisfaction in the fact that John D. Rockefeller, the richest man in the world, is compelled to breakfast on a diluted glass of milk. But regrettable or no, Lord Stranleigh of Wychwood was preparing to do full justice to the excellence of the meal when his man said to him, in a hushed, deferential whisper:

"Mr. Peter Mackeller has called, my lord, and insists on seeing you immediately. He says it is a matter of the utmost importance."

"Oh, dim!" ejaculated his lordship, "how these conscientious, earnest people tire me. As if anything could be a matter of importance at this hour except breakfast! Well, I suppose there is no escape: show him in."

He heaved a deep sigh, and murmured to himself:

"This is what comes of meddling with the city." The stalwart young Mackeller entered, and his very presence seemed to put the refined room to shame, his grim force causing his surroundings to appear *dilettante* and needlessly expensive. He was even more than usually unkempt, as if he had been sitting up all night in the hold of the tramp steamer which had kidnapped him. A deep frown marked his brow, and heightened the expression of rude strength that radiated from his determined face.

"Ah, Mackeller, good morning," drawled his lordship, looking at the young man over his shoulder. "I'm delighted to see you, and just in the nick of time, too. Won't you sit down and breakfast with me!"

"Thank you," said Mackeller, in tones as hard as the other's were affected. "I breakfasted two hours and a half ago."

"Did you really? Well, call it lunch, and draw up your chair."

"No, I've not come to a banquet, but to a business conference."

"I'm sorry for that. My head is not very clear on business matters at any hour of the day, but in the morning I am particularly stupid. Do try a peach; you'll find them exceedingly good."

"No, thanks."

"Then have a cigarette?"

His lordship raised the heavy lid of a richly chased box of silver, displaying a quantity of the paper tubes, and pushed this toward his visitor.

"They are a blend that is made for me in Cairo, but perhaps you prefer Virginians?"

"I have no choice in the matter," said Mackeller, selecting a cigarette.

The butler snapped aglow an electric lighter, and held it convenient for the young engineer's use, who drew in his breath, and exhaled a whiff of aromatic smoke.

"Do sit down, Mackeller!"

"Thanks, no; I'm in a hurry. Time is of great value just now."

"Although I am very stupid in the morning, as I told you, nevertheless the moment you came in I surmised you were in a hurry. For whom are you working, Mr. Mackeller?"

"Working? What do you mean?"

"Who is your employer, or are you on your own, as the vulgar say?"

"Why, my lord, I understood I was in your employ."

"In that case why don't you sit down when I tell you to?" asked his lordship with a slight laugh.

Peter Mackeller dropped into a chair with such suddenness that the laugh of his chief became more pronounced.

"You see, Peter, my boy, it is a rule of the world that the man who pays for the music calls the tune. You say it is to be a quick-step: I insist upon a minuet. How do you like those cigarettes?"

"They are excellent, my lord."

"Not half bad, I think. You don't mind my going on with breakfast, and I am sure you will excuse me if I fail to regard this table as a quick lunch counter. I think our sturdiness as a nation depends very largely on our slowness at meals."

"Perhaps. Still, that slowness should not extend to every function of life," replied Peter severely.

"You think not? Well, perhaps you are right, although I must confess that I do dislike to be hustled, as the saying is. My mind works slowly when it condescends to work at all, and my body rather accommodates itself to my mental condition. You appear to be under the impression that my affairs at the moment need the spur rather than the curb. Am I right in that conjecture?"

"Why, my lord, if ever there was a transaction where speed is the essence of the contract, as the lawyers say, it is the present condition of your gold property."

"Why, I fail to see that, Mackeller. I buy a property for, say, thirty-five thousand pounds. I receive a check for sixty-five thousand from the estimable Mr. Schwartzbrod and his colleagues. I have therefore acquired what you state is a valuable property for nothing, and there is bestowed upon me a bonus of thirty thousand pounds in addition for taking it over. Whether or not any gold exists on the west coast of Africa, there certainly reposes thirty thousand golden sovereigns at my disposal in the bank; sovereigns which yesterday I did not possess, so I think I have concluded the deal very creditably for a sluggish-brained person like myself, and after such a profitable bit of mental exertion it seems to me I am entitled to a rest, but here you come, bristling with energy, and say 'Let's hurry.' In Heaven's name, why? I've finished the transaction."

"Finished?" cried Mackeller. "Finished? Bless my soul, we've only just begun. Do you understand that the tramp steamer *Rajah,* with some hundred and fifty hired thieves aboard, is making as fast as steam can push her through the waters, for your property, with intent to loot the same? Do you comprehend that that steamer has been loaded by myself with the most modern surface-mining machinery, with dynamite, with provisions, with every facility for the speedy robbing of those gold fields, and that you have given that pirate Schwartzbrod a document acquitting him of all liability in the premises?"

"Yes, Peter, I suppose things are very much as you state them, but your tone implies that somehow I am to blame in the matter. I assure you that it is not my fault, but the fault of circumstances. Then why worry about a thing I am not in the least responsible for? You are not censuring me, I hope?"

"No, my lord, I have no right to censure you whatever happens."

"Oh, don't let any question of right suppress a just indignation, Mackeller. If you think I'm guilty of negligence, pray give expression to your feelings by the use of any combination of words that brings relief. Don't mind me. I really very much admire the use of terse language, although I have been denied the gift of emphatic denunciation myself."

"Don't you intend to do anything, my lord?"

"Yes, I intend to enjoy my breakfast, and really, if you knew how tasty this coffee is, you would yield to my pleadings and indulge in at least one cup."

"Don't you propose to prosecute that scoundrel Schwartzbrod?"

"Prosecute? Bless my soul, what for?"

"For the trick he played on you and my father. He got that exculpating document from you under false pretenses."

"Not at all, not at all. I made certain stipulations; he complied with them. I then gave him the exculpating document, as you call it, and there it ends. If I had been gifted with second sight, this vision would have revealed to me that the clever Schwartzbrod had caused the *Rajah* to sail with you a prisoner in her hold. But Schwartzbrod is not to blame because I possess no clairvoyant power, now is he?"

"You will do nothing, then?"

"My dear boy, there's nothing to do."

"Don't you intend to stop these pirates from mining your gold, and getting it aboard the *Rajah?*"

"Certainly not: why should I?"

"Nor give information to the authorities?"

"Of course not. The authorities have more information now than they can use."

"Then you will not even tell the police?"

"The police are a land force: they cannot take a rowboat and chase the *Rajah,* and if they could they wouldn't catch her, so what's the good of asking impossibilities from either Scotland Yard or the Foreign Office?"

"You have no intention, then, of interfering with this band of gold robbers?"

"Oh, no."

"You're going to take it lying down?"

"No, sitting up," and with that his lordship pushed back his chair, threw his right leg over his left, selected a cigarette, and lit it.

"I should be glad, my lord, to head an expedition, fit up another ship, follow the *Rajah,* and force those claim-jumpers to abandon their raid on another man's goods."

"I don't like force, Mackeller. I don't mind possessing a giant's strength, but we must remember we should not use it like a giant."

Lord Stranleigh, a picture of contentment, leaned back in his chair, and blew rings of filmy cigarette smoke toward the ceiling. Peter Mae-keller, the gloom on whose face had grown darker and darker, watched the nonchalant young man opposite him with a curl of contempt on his lip, yet he realized that if his lordship could not be forced to move, he himself was helpless. At last he rose slowly to his feet, the first tardy movement he had made since he entered the breakfast room.

"Very good, my lord. Then you have no further need of me, and I beg you to accept my resignation."

"I'm sorry," drawled his lordship, "but before you quit my service, I should like to receive one well thought-out opinion from you."

"What is your problem, my lord?"

"It is this, Mackeller. I consider the after-breakfast cigarette the most enticing smoke of the day. A man who has slept well, and breakfasted adequately seems just in tune to enjoy to the utmost these enchanting vaporous exhalations. I wish to know if you agree with me."

"Oh, damnation!" cried Mackeller, bringing his huge fist down on the table, and setting the breakfast things a-jingling, and with this regrettable word and action, he strode toward the door. The butler was there as if to open it for him, but his lordship made a slight turning motion of his wrist, whereupon Ponderby instantly locked the door and put the key in his pocket, standing there as silent and imperturbable as if he had not just imprisoned a free-born British subject, which he certainly had no legal right to do. The enraged captive fruitlessly shook the door, then turned round, his face ablaze with anger. Neither his lordship nor the butler moved a muscle.

"Mr. Mackeller," drawled his lordship, "you have been conversing most interestingly, I admit, on subjects that did not in the least concern you. Now, perhaps, you will resume your duty."

"My duty? What is my duty?" demanded the engineer.

"Why, I hoped it would not be necessary to remind you of it. I sent you down to Southampton to look after my property; the *Rajah*, which I had hired, and the machinery, provisions, etcetera, which I had bought. Through your negligence, carelessness, laches, default, supineness, inattention, or whatever other quality it pleases you to attribute the circumstance, you allowed yourself to be hoodwinked like a schoolboy, trapped like a rat, tied like a helpless sack on a pack horse for an unstated number of miles, flung like a bundle into a pilot boat, and landed like a haddock on the beach. A man to whom all this happened must be well endowed with cheek to enter my house and berate me for indolence. So cease standing there like a graven image with your back to the door, and do not perambulate the room as you did a minute ago, like a tiger in his cage at the Zoo, but sit down here once more, light another cigarette, fling one leg over the other, and give me, slowly, so that I can understand it, a formal report of your Southampton mission, and the disaster which attended it. I shall be glad to receive and consider any excuse you may offer for your own utter incompetence, and you may begin by apologizing for dealing a deadly blow at my table, which is quite innocent, and for offending my ears by the expletive that preceded such action."

Mackeller strode over to the chair again, and plumped down like the fall of a sledge-hammer.

"You're right. I apologize, and ask you to pardon my tongue-play and fist-play."

His lordship airily waved his hand.

"Granted," he said. "I sometimes say 'dim' myself, if I may quote Sir W. S. Gilbert. Go on."

"When I went aboard the *Rajah*, neither the captain nor any of the officers offered opposition to my resuming command of the loading. The stuff was on the wharf, and in less than three days it was all aboard, well stowed away. During this time I had seen nothing to rouse my suspicion that anything underhand was to be attempted. I had informed the captain that you were now the charterer of the steamer, and he received the intelligence with apparent indifference, saying something to the effect that it mattered nothing to him who his owners were so long as his money was safe. The last material taken aboard was a large quantity of canvas for making tents, and lucky for me it was that I placed this at the foot of the ladder up from the hold. The workers had all gone on deck, and I was taking a final look around, wondering whether anything had been forgotten. I then mounted the ladder, and was amazed to see old Schwartzbrod standing there, talking to a tall, dark man who was, I afterwards learned, the leader of the expedition. This man, without a word, planted his foot against my breast, and heaved me backward down into the hold. Immediately afterwards I was battened down, and in darkness. By the running about on the deck above me, I realized that the steamer was getting ready to cast off, and within an hour I heard the engines and screw at work.

"It was night, and we were thrashing seaward through the Channel when the covering of the hatchway was lifted, and the man who had imprisoned me came down the ladder alone, with a lantern in his hand, which struck me as rather brave in the circumstances, but then he was armed, and I was not, so after all I had little chance against him. He placed the lantern on the bales of canvas upon which I had fallen, and began, with seeming courtesy, by begging pardon for what he had done. Throughout he spoke very quietly, and impressed me as a determined and capable person. He said that if I gave him my word that I should speak to no one aboard, or attempt to hail any passing craft, should such come near us, he would allow me on deck, and would send me ashore when the pilot left the ship.

"'And if I refuse to give my word?' I asked. "' In that case,' he replied, 'I shall supply you with food and water, and will carry you to the end of our voyage.'

"'And where is that?' I asked.

"'I don't know,' he said. 'I have nothing to do with the navigation of the ship. I believe we are making for some port in South America, but I couldn't say for certain.'

"I realized that I could do nothing while in the hold, and although I knew perfectly well they were making for the West African coast, and not for South America, I would be equally helpless once I reached there. Besides, it was of vital importance that I should telegraph to you and my father. In fact, I was amazed that, having taken the risk of placing me in confinement as they had done, they should allow me to get on shore so soon, but I suppose the crafty old Schwartzbrod knew that if I remained missing long, there would be an outcry in the newspapers, so he reckoned it was safer to risk my being put ashore, as he estimated we could not possibly fit out another steamer and start in pursuit under a week at the very least, and with that start they could have the channel of the river blocked, a fort or two erected, and so bid us defiance when we did arrive."

"But if they blocked the river," interrupted his lordship, "they would shut themselves in, as well as shut us out."

"Not necessarily," continued the engineer. "I have reason to believe that before I reached Southampton, a number of floating mines were stowed away in the front part of the ship. These mines could be planted in the mouth of the river, and a chart kept, which, in the possession of the captain, would enable him to thread the channel in safety, while a navigator without this protection and guide would run a thousand chances of finding his ship blown up."

"Why," said his lordship with admiration, "our seven syndicaters are brave as the buccaneers of ancient times. They are certainly running considerable risk of penal servitude for life?"

"I am not sure that they are, my lord," replied Mackeller. "You see, this property is situated in a native state. The concession was granted by the chief of the ruling tribe in that district. British law does not run in that locality, and I very much doubt if the steamer *Rajah* will ever again put into a British port. My notion is that they will load her up with ore, and make for some point, probably in the Portuguese possessions, where they will smelt the ore, sell the ingots, and in the shape of hard cash which cannot be earmarked, the product of your mine will reach the syndicate in London. Now, my lord, you spoke of negligence, culpability, and all that. There is the story, and if you can show me where I was negligent of your interests, all I can say is that my error was not intentional."

"Well, you see, Mackeller, you were acquainted with old Schwartzbrod, and I wasn't. I had not met him up to that time, and I knew nothing personally of the syndicate, whereas you did. I think you should have put some shrewd man on to watch the trains, and learn if any of these men had come to Southampton, or perhaps you should have given us the tip in London, and we could have had the immaculate seven shadowed. I expected to meet legal chicanery, but not bold swashbuckling of this sort."

"Yes, it would have been better to set a watch, but although I knew the men, nothing in their conduct led me to suspect a trick like this. However, as I am no longer in your employ, you shall not suffer further from my incompetence."

"I think, Maekeller, you ought to give me a week's notice, you know."

"Very well. This day week I quit."

"I am not sure but I am entitled to a month. How much should I have to pay you if I dismissed you?"

"Six months' salary, I believe, is the legal amount."

"Well, then, why not give me half a year's notice?"

"I suppose you are entitled to it, my lord."

"Then that's all right. Half a year from now we shake hands and bid each other a tearful farewell. Much may happen in twenty-six weeks, you know."

"Not if you're going to do nothing, Lord Stranleigh."

"Maekeller, you may not be a thing of beauty, but you are a joy forever. Still, there is one characteristic which I do not like about you. Perhaps it is oversensitiveness on my part, but it sometimes seems to me that you think I am lacking in energy. I hope, however, I am mistaken." His lordship paused and gazed with quaint anxiety at his visitor, who, however, made no response, whereupon his lordship sighed ever so slightly, and put on the look of patient resignation which becomes a misunderstood man.

"Silence gives consent, I think, and I may find it difficult to put your mind right on this subject. Let me give you an illustration, chosen from your own interesting profession of mining engineering. I am credibly informed that if a hole is drilled in a piece of hard rock, and a portion of dynamite inserted therein, the explosion which follows generally rends the rock in twain." Again he paused, and again there was no reply. It was but too evident that the serious Mackeller considered himself being trifled with. Unabashed, his lordship proceeded:

"That is energy, if you like. Shall we name it Mackellerite—this form of energy? Now I shall tell you of a thing I have seen done on one of my own estates. A number of holes were bored in a large bowlder, and instead of dynamite, we drove in a number of wooden pins, and over those pins we placidly poured clear, cold water. After a time the rock gently parted. There was no dust, no smoke, no flame and fury and nerve-shattering detonation, yet the swelling pins had done exactly the same work that your stick of dynamite would have performed. Now, that also was energy, of the Stranleighite variety. I suppose it would be difficult to make the stick of dynamite understand the stick of wood, and vice versa. By the way, have you seen your father since you returned from Southampton!"

"Yes."

"Did he tell you I possess a trim little oceangoing steam yacht at present lying in a British harbor!"

"No, he did not."

"But I thought I made him aware of what I intended to do!"

"Apparently he understood you no better than I do; at least he told me he did not know what course you proposed to take."

"I informed him that my yacht was fitted out with turbine engines, and could reel off, at a pinch, twenty-five knots an hour. Now, how far away is this bally gold property of yours!"

"About three thousand five hundred miles."

"Very good. Toward this interesting spot the *Rajah* is plodding along at seven knots an hour, perhaps doing a little less, as her owners guarantee that speed. How long will it take her to reach the what-do-you-call-it river? There is no use of my attempting figures when I have an uncivil engineer in my employ."

"About twenty-one days," replied Mackeller.

"Very well. If my yacht goes only twice that speed, which she can accomplish in her sleep, we'd get there in half the time, wouldn't we? I think that mathematical calculation is correct?"

"Yes, it is."

"Then we'd be Johnnie-on-the-spot in about eleven days, wouldn't we?"

"Yes, my lord."

"The *Rajah* has now four days the start of us. Then don't you see we can spend six more days over our porridge in the morning, and still reach our river before she does? Now don't you begin to be ashamed of yourself, Mackeller? Why rush me over my frugal meal when we have such ample time to spare? I'd much rather spend the six days here in London than up some malarious alligator-filled river on the west coast of Africa." Mackeller's stern face brightened.

"Then you do intend to chase them, after all, my lord?"

"Chase them? Lord bless you, no. Why should I chase them? They are the good Schwartzbrod's hired men. He's paying their wages. Chase them? Of course not; but I'm going to pass them, and get up the river before they do."

Mackeller sprang to his feet, his face ablaze with enthusiasm, his right fist nervously clenching and unclenching.

"Now, do sit down, Peter," wailed his lordship. "Do not let us display unnecessary energy. I've told you two or three times I don't like it."

Peter sat down.

"What I was trying to do when you went off prematurely was to show you the folly of underestimating a fellow creature. You come storming in here, practically accusing me of doing nothing, whereas I am doing nothing because everything is done, and you, on the rampage, have arrived from a total and grotesque failure."

"I apologized for that already, my lord."

"So you did, Peter. I had forgotten. A man shouldn't be asked to pay twice for the same horse and cart, should he? Ponderby," he continued, turning to his impassive butler, "would you be so good as to go into my business office, and bring me my telegraph duplicate book."

Then, turning to his visitor, he added:

"I am so methodical that I keep a copy of every telegram I send. I shall ask you to look through this book with the critical eye of an engineer, and you will learn that while you were raging up from Plymouth I was ordering by telegraph to be sent to my yacht the more important materials for the contest in which we may be involved. A man must make some move to protect his own property, you know."

"Why, my lord, that's just what I've been saying all along, but you gave me to understand you were going to do nothing."

"I cannot account for such an idea arising in your mind. I think you must have jumped at conclusions, Mackeller. Still, as long as I can convince you that I am really a practical man, everything will be all right between us."

The butler placed before Lord Stranleigh the book containing copies of the telegrams sent the day before, and his lordship handed it gracefully to Mackeller.

"Nothing like documentary evidence," he said, "to convince a stubborn man. I think even you will admit that I have risen to the occasion." Mackeller turned the leaves of the book, reading as he went along. His eyebrows came lower and lower over his gloomy eyes, and a faint smile moved the lips of his lordship as he sat there watching him. Finally, he snapped the book shut, and put it down with a slap on the table.

"Twenty-four dozens of champagne; fifty dozens of claret, burgundy, bock, Scotch whisky — —"

"Oh, and Irish whisky, too," interrupted his lordship eagerly. "I haven't forgotten anything, you know. You see, I have some Irish blood in my veins, and I occasionally touch it up with a little of the national brew."

"I don't think your blood needs any stimulation," said Mackeller dejectedly. "Here you have ordered tobacco by the hundredweight, pipes by the score, cigars and cigarettes by the thousand. I suppose you think there's something funny in handing me these messages. Are you never in earnest, my lord?"

"Never more so than at the present moment, Mackeller. I am disappointed that you failed to detect genius in the commissariat."

"Are you going to fight this band of ruffians, my lord, by popping champagne corks at them, or smothering them in tobacco smoke?"

"I have told you once or twice, Mackeller, that I don't intend fighting any one at all, but if the band of ruffians should come to dine with me aboard the yacht, I'd like the hospitality shown them to do me credit."

"Very well, your lordship," said Peter with resignation. "You have reminded me that my time is not my own, but yours, so if it gives you any pleasure to befool me, don't allow consideration for my feelings to retard you."

"Ah, you got in a good left-hander on me there, Peter. That's where you score. Now, the proper time having elapsed after a meal when a man should talk business, even if, like me, he does not understand it, he can at least pretend to be wise, no matter how foolish, he is in reality. What is the name of that river of yours again?"

"The Paramakaboo."

"Thanks. Well, as I understood you, it reaches the sea by several channels. Is our property on the main stream?"

"The streams are all about the same size, so far as I was able to learn."

"How far back from the coast are the mountains?"

"You can hardly call them mountains. They are reasonably high hills, and I estimate the distance to be from twenty-five to thirty miles. Our property is twelve miles up the river."

"A steamer drawing the depth of the Rajah could get up there you think?"

"Oh, yes, and could lay alongside the rocks in front of the gold field without needing a wharf of any sort."

"If I took the yacht up another channel, would she be out of sight of any one stationed on our property?"

"The delta is rather flat for a few miles back from the coast, but if you go upstream for fifteen miles or so, there are plenty of hills that would conceal even a line of battle-ship, but any one on your property could see her sailing up the stream while she was in low-lying country."

"That doesn't matter. I intend to get there before our friends do, so there will be no trouble on that score."

"Don't you intend to arm your yacht?"

"Oh, yes; I shall have on board a few sporting rifles, some shotguns, and plenty of ammunition. Is there any game back in the mountains?"

"I don't know. How many riflemen do you propose to take with you?"

"I was thinking of inviting some of my younger gamekeepers; perhaps half a dozen."

"But they can't hold out against a hundred and fifty well-armed men, not to mention the sailors belonging to the *Rajah*."

"My dear fellow, why is your mind always running on fighting? This is no Treasure Island cruise, with stockades, and one-legged John Silver, and that sort of thing. We are not qualifying for literary immortality, not being filibusters, but merely staid, respectable city persons going to look over a property we have purchased. If we are discovered and attacked, we will valorously fly, and as, at a pinch, I can get twenty-five knots an hour out of the boat, I think with the current of the stream in my favor we can reach the sea in case these misguided persons become obstreperous. You forget that as a city man I am an investor, not a speculator."

"I don't see how that course of action will save your gold from being stolen."

"Don't you? Well, you'll have an inkling by and by. Now, I wish you to go back to Southampton. You negotiated for the charter of the *Rajah*, I believe."

"Yes."

"Who are her owners?"

"Messrs. Sparling & Bilge."

"Very well. I'll give you a blank check and ask you to return to Southampton. Discover, if you can, what is the reasonable value of the *Rajah*, then go to Sparling & Bilge and purchase the steamer. See that everything is done legally, and arrange the transfer to me."

"Is there to be any limit in the price I am to pay, Lord Stranleigh?"

"Oh, yes, of course we must place a limit; say ten times the value of the ship. Make as good a bargain as you can. Part of the arrangement must be that Sparling & Bilge write a letter to the captain, telling him that they have sold the boat, that it belongs to me, and that they have transferred to me whatever contract they made with him, the officers and the crew; that I will be responsible hereafter for the pay of the same. Then find out what can be done toward changing the name of the steamer. I wish to paint out the word *Rajah* and substitute, out of compliment to you, the name *Blue Peter*. Blue Peter means the flag of that color with a white square which is run up to the masthead when the ship is about to sail, and I doubt not the Blue Peter was flying over Peter Mackeller as he lay in the hold. Please learn if we can change the name legally, and if we cannot, why, we'll see what can be done when the ship is in our possession. I am not going to indulge in any amateur piracy, so I expect you to look sharply after the legal points of the transfer. Get the assistance of the best marine lawyer there is in Southampton. Do you understand what I mean?"

"Yes, my lord, and I will carry out your instructions to the letter. I think I see what you intend to do."

"I am the most transparent of men, Mackeller. There's no subtlety about me, so you can gain little credit by fathoming my plans. We will suppose that two days are required to put me in possession of the *Rajah*. Return then to London, pack your trunk, bid good-by to all your friends, and say nothing to them of what you have done, or what you intend to do, what you guess, or what you know, not even to your father, whom I have made president of the company, because I dislike unnecessary publicity, and desire to keep my name in the shade of that modest obscurity which has always enveloped it. Buy anything you think you may require for the voyage, and ship your dunnage to Plymouth, addressed, care of the yacht, *The Woman in White*. Then engage a berth in the sleeping car on the 9.50 Penzance express, Great Western Railway, first-class fare, and five shillings extra for your stateroom, and don't forget to charge it to me. At the unholy hour of 6.49 in the morning, you will arrive at Redruth in Cornwall, where you can indulge in an early breakfast, which you seem to delight in. In the environs of that village you will find a little property which is owned by me, and on that bit of land is an abandoned copper mine with a smelting furnace. I think the smelting apparatus is in reasonably good order, but I doubt if any of the other appurtenances of the mine are of much value. Now, having gone into the mining business, I intend to work this property for all it's worth, and I propose that you spend a day or two getting a suitable manager, rigging up windlasses, and that sort of thing, so that we will see whether there is more money in copper to-day than was the case when the mine was abandoned, years and years ago. I suppose that modern processes may enable us to extract more copper out of the ore than our fathers found possible. Anyhow, my idea is to get the blast furnace in working order once more, and by the time we return to England, we shall probably know whether there is any brass, in another sense of the word, in the mine. Do you think you comprehend that task as well as the buying of the— —

"But why trouble with copper, Lord Stranleigh, when you have on your hands the most prolific gold mine, as I believe it to be, in the world?"

"You said it was in the other fellow's hands, Mackeller."

"Don't you intend to stop that crew in some way from lifting the ore?"

"Oh, no, I shall not interfere with them in the least."

"Then what are you going to West Africa for?"

"For the voyage. For the scenery. For the chance of big game in the back country. To drink some of that champagne I have ordered, and to smoke a few of those cigarettes which I sent aboard. I shall read all the latest books that I haven't had time to peruse here in London. By the way, is the neighborhood of our mine a healthy locality?"

"I should say it was rather feverish along the coast, but up toward the hills I think it as healthy as Hampstead."

"I shall induce a doctor friend of mine to come with us. I'm glad I thought of that. If you indulge in your predilection for coercion, giving free rein to your passion for fighting, a surgeon will be necessary for amputations, the dressing of wounds, and generally useful in attending to those exciting incidents that follow in the train of a conqueror like yourself, who believes in brute force rather than in alert brains."

"Then I am to set this copper mine of yours in operation down in Cornwall?"

"Exactly. And leave a competent manager to engage the men, renew the machinery, and all that."

"Is there to be any limit in the expenditure?"

"Limit? Of course there is to be a limit. Aren't we always limiting expenditure? Isn't my life spent in putting a check on the outgoings? Yes, you will instruct the new manager that this is merely a tentative experiment of mine, and that he is not to purchase machinery wholesale, nor engage many miners, but merely to test the capabilities of the copper vein, and smelt as much of the ore as he can until you return."

"Of course it's no business of mine, my lord, but it strikes me that this is an unnecessary and losing venture. The copper industry of Cornwall has been steadily decreasing in value, and I doubt if there are half as many copper mines in operation as there were ten years ago."

"Oh, Peter, Peter, how little of the foresight of your saintly namesake do you possess! Does not your imagination see the little harbor of Portreath, which means the sandy cove? Of course it doesn't, for you are probably ignorant that such a port exists. Our smelter is situated near this marine haven of rest. Stir up your fancy, my boy, and see in your mind's eye the steamer *Rajah,* loaded with ore, but renamed the *Blue Peter,* floating majestically into Portreath. What more natural than that the grasping Stranleigh should own another copper mine where there is no smelter, and that this ship brings copper ore to our Cornwall furnace? The *Blue Peter* shall probably first put into Plymouth, where she is less likely to be recognized by seafaring folk than would be the case at Southampton. We will there discharge the crew, giving every man double pay. We will compensate the captain and his officers, sending everybody away happy. Then we will engage another captain and another crew, who know nothing of where the steamer has come from, and thus we sail round Land's End, and put in to little Portreath."

"You propose, then, to capture the *Rajah* on the high seas, following it with your much more speedy yacht?"

"Oh, no, not capture. I'm going to take possession, that's all. The *Rajah* is mine as incontestably as the yacht is. The ore with which she will be loaded is also mine. Everything shall be done as legally as if we were transacting our affairs in the Temple or Gray's Inn. Doesn't that put to shame your wild Scottish Highland ideas of fighting and slaughter? You ought to wear kilts and a dirk, Mackeller, but my instrument is a quill pen and nice red stamps embossed at Somerset House."

"And who will pay the men who are blasting out the ore on the banks of the river Paramakaboo?"

"Why, really, Mackeller, that is no affair of mine. These industrious people are employed by the saintly Schwartzbrod. If that astute financier elects to engage a large body of labor to get out my ore for me, then I think you will admit, Mackeller, much as you are prejudiced against him, that he is really the philanthropic benefactor of his race I have always said he was."

"But—but—but," stammered Mackeller, "when they discover how they have been befooled, there will be a riot."

"I don't see that. When I discharge the captain and crew at Plymouth, I shall have cut the live wire, if I may use an expression from your absorbing profession. The connecting cable between those deluded miners in West Africa and the amiable syndicate in London, will be severed. The captain knows nothing, I take it, of Schwartzbrod. He was employed by Sparling & Bilge. Going ashore at Plymouth, out of a job, he would probably look for a ship in that port, and failing to find one, might journey to his old employers at Southampton. But, although I discharge the captain, I don't intend to turn him adrift. I have already set influences at work which will secure for him a better boat than the *Rajah*, and the contented man will sail away from Plymouth, from London, or from some northern port, as the case may be. It is not likely that captain, officers, or crew know the nature of the ore they will be carrying, but I don't intend to leave the wire partially cut. I shall provide places on various ships for officers and crew, and scatter them over the face of the earth, casting my breadwinners on the waters, as one may say, hoping they will not return for many days."

"But when Schwartzbrod hears nothing of the *Rajah* at whatever foreign port he ordered her to sail, he will make inquiries of Sparling & Bilge."

"I very much doubt that."

"Why?"

"Because he has chartered their ship, and must either produce the steamer or renew the charter. That reminds me, for how long a period was the *Rajah* engaged?"

"For three months with option of renewal."

"Good. Toward the end of that time old Schwartzbrod will write to Sparling & Bilge extending the charter for another three months. He dare not go to see these shipping men because he has mislaid their steamship, and does not wish to answer embarrassing questions regarding her whereabouts."

"Yes, but Sparling & Bilge will merely reply that they have sold the *Rajah* to Lord Stran-leigh, and beg to refer Schwartzbrod to the new owner."

"Bravo, Peter. You are actually beginning to get an inkling of Mr. Schwartzbrod's dilemma. I had almost despaired of making this clear to you."

"Still, I don't understand the object of cutting the live wire, as you call it, if you leave another communicating wire intact. You take great pains to prevent captain or any of the crew meeting Schwartzbrod, yet you make it inevitable that Schwartzbrod will learn you are the owner of the *Rajah*. Perhaps you wish me to pledge Sparling & Bilge to secrecy?"

"Oh, dear no. I anticipate great pleasure in meeting Mr. Schwartzbrod. I picture him cringing and bowing and rubbing one hand over the other as he pleads for a renewal of the charter, and crawls away from all my inquiries regarding the whereabouts of the steamer. I will be back in London by the time the syndicate begins to get uneasy about the *Rajah*, and I shall renew the charter with the utmost cheerfulness, without insisting on learning where the *Rajah* is. But imagine the somewhat delicate position of a man compelled to negotiate with me for the hire of a boat to steal my own gold. The venerable Schwartzbrod will need to keep a close guard on his tongue or he will give himself away. It is a delicious dilemma. I hope you comprehend all the possibilities of the situation, but be that as it may, get you off to Southampton, and when you are done with the copper mine, report on board my yacht at Plymouth, where you will find me waiting for you. Then for the blue sea and red carnage if it is so written. Sixteen men on a dead man's chest, yo, ho, ho, and a bottle of champagne, and all that sort of thing, Peter."

CHAPTER IV—THE MAGNET OF THE GOLD FIELD

THE young and energetic Mackeller completed his purchase of the steamer *Rajah* in something less than three hours, instead of taking the two days which Lord Stranleigh had allowed him. It is very easy to buy a ship in Southampton if you happen to have the money about you. An excellent express on the South Western line whisked him up to London again, and he spent the afternoon in securing what he needed for the long voyage that was ahead of him, dispatching his purchases, as his lordship had directed, to the care of the yacht at Plymouth. As his acquaintance with Lord Stranleigh progressed, his first impression of the lord of Wychwood became considerably modified. In spite of the young nobleman's airy, nonchalant manner in speaking of what the young engineer regarded as serious subjects, Mackeller began slowly to realize that there was thought and method behind all this persiflage which he so much disliked, and he began to doubt his theory that Stranleigh's successful encounter with the syndicate had been merely a fluke, as, at first, he had supposed. The plan his lordship so sketchily outlined, of regaining his own property on the high seas, struck the practical mind of Mackeller as probably feasible, but although all the legality would be on his lordship's side; although his opponents were engaged in a gigantic scheme of barefaced robbery, nevertheless, Mackeller had knocked about at the ends of the earth too much to be ignorant of the fact that in certain quarters of the globe lawfulness of action was but a minor point in the game. Indeed, the law-abiding citizen was at a distinct disadvantage unless he held superior force at his command to compel rather than to persuade. There is little use in arguing with a man who holds a loaded revolver, so on one point Lord Stranleigh failed to convince his subordinate. Mackeller thought it folly to proceed to West Africa with a small body of men, and no more persuasive ammunition than champagne and cigarettes. Therefore, in purchasing his own equipment Mackeller took the precaution of buying a dozen of the latest repeating rifles, with many thousand cartridges to fit the same, and this battery he ordered forwarded to the yacht to supplement whatever sporting guns Lord Stranleigh provided for the gamekeepers and foresters whom he took with him. Mackeller believed that these would be stanch, stubborn, capable young men, and although few in number, they might, if well armed, put the rabble of a hundred and fifty to flight, should a contest arise.

The dark man who kicked Mackeller downstairs into the hold, and who afterwards interviewed him alone by lantern light, had impressed Mackeller as being a capable leader of men, and he would probably drill his following into some sort of shape during the long voyage to the south. That the captain, officers, and crew, or any of the hundred and fifty knew the piratical nature of the expedition, Mackeller very strongly doubted, but the prompt manner in which the leader, with his energetic foot, broke the law, and very nearly broke Mackeller's neck, convinced the engineer that the dark man was well aware of the criminal nature of his proceeding, and undoubtedly, when once the force was landed, he would be very much on the alert, expecting that as soon as the flight of the steamer became known, instant arrangements would be made for pursuit. He would doubtless send out scouts, and endeavor roughly to understand the lay of the land on which he found himself. It was morally certain, thought Mackeller, that one or other of those scouts would ultimately come upon the yacht, no matter how securely they hid her, and so soon as her presence came to the knowledge of the strenuous leader of the filibusters, an attack on the yacht was certain, and her capture or destruction most probable, unless they could escape quickly to the open sea. So, as Mackeller knew there were no gun shops along the Paramakaboo River, he took precaution to make provision beforehand without saying anything to his peace-loving master. A man whose daily walk is Piccadilly is scarcely in a position to predict what may happen on the Paramakaboo.

At 9.50 that night Mackeller was in occupation of his most comfortable little room in the sleeping car of the Penzance express, and an excellent night's rest followed his busy day. Seven o'clock next morning found him at breakfast in Redruth, and so resolutely did he go about his business that in two days he formed complete the organization which was to operate the old copper mine. Then he took train for Plymouth, and was rowed out in the evening to the white yacht at anchor in the harbor, resting beautiful as a swan on the placid waters. Mackeller was astonished to find her so great a boat. She was almost as large as the *Rajah*, but of much more dainty shape, her fine lines giving promise of great speed. Thin cables, extending from slanting mast to slanting mast, he recognized as the outside paraphernalia for wireless telegraphy, and although he saw from this that Lord Stranleigh treated himself to the latest scientific inventions, he was quite unprepared for the quiet luxury that everywhere met his eye once he was aboard of the yacht.

He found Lord Stranleigh aft, seated in a cane chair, his feet resting on another. He had been reading the latest evening paper brought aboard, and he laid this on his knee as he looked lazily up at his mining engineer.

"Finished with copper, Mackeller?" he asked. "Yes, my lord."

"I did not expect you before to-morrow night. I imagine, you gave your disconcerting energy full play down in Cornwall."

"I have been reasonably busy, my lord."

"Would you mind pressing that electrical button? It is just out of my reach."

Mackeller did so, and a cabin boy immediately put in an appearance.

"Go forward, and ask Captain Wilkie if he will be good enough to allow me a word with him." Captain Wilkie proved to be a grizzled old sea-dog of unmistakably Scotch extraction. He rolled aft, and saluted his owner.

"Everything ready, captain?"

"Everything ready, sir."

"Very well; up anchor and away."

The captain went forward and mounted the bridge.

"Draw up your chair, Peter, and let me have your verbal report, and as you drop into the chair, drop also that appellation 'my lord.' If you want to be extra respectful at any time, say 'sir' as the captain does, and I'll do the same by you, if you require it."

Mackeller gave him a full account of his occupation during the last three days, but whether Stranleigh was asleep or not throughout the recital, he could not be sure. At any rate he did not interrupt, but lay back in his chair with closed eyes. Then, without opening them, he remarked:

"You have done very well, Mackeller, and as a reward I will give you the choice of a spot in the Bay of Biscay or the Atlantic Ocean where you may wish your case of rifles and ammunition heaved overboard."

"Oh, have you been examining my dunnage, sir?" asked Mackeller.

"Dear me, no," replied Stranleigh languidly. "Your fool of a gunsmith did not understand your instructions, and not knowing where to find you, and supposing you were acting for me, he telegraphed asking which of two rifles named should be sent. Learning that twelve had been ordered, I thought of telegraphing in the old phrase, 'Six of one and half a dozen of the other,' but I finally took on a score altogether, ten of each kind with ammunition to match."

"Why purchase more guns than I did, if you're going to drop them in the Bay of Biscay."

"Oh, they'll make the bigger plump when they go down."

"What harm will they do aboard, sir? If we don't need them, we won't use them. If we do need them, then you'll be sorry they're in the Bay of Biscay."

"So you're going to choose the Bay of Biscay, are you? I thought perhaps you might toss them over farther along than that. I hope you understand, Mackeller, I am on a mission of peace, and if, for any reason, the yacht should be searched, your rifles and ammunition would be rather a giveaway, wouldn't they?"

"I don't see that. You've got more than a score of men aboard here, and the repeaters can be used for sporting purposes."

"All right, Mackeller, don't be alarmed. The boxes are stowed safely away in the forrard hold, and we'll not drop them overboard anywhere. After all, you know the locality for which we are bound better than I do, and so your rifles and ammunition may prove friends in need. I see the boy hovering about in the offing, and I am sure he wishes to conduct you to your cabin. By the time you've washed the railway dust from your sylphlike form, the dinner gong will be filling the air with a welcome melody. I've got my own favorite chef with me, and I understand we shall not need to live on porridge and tinned milk. And, by the way, Mackeller, did you happen to pack such wearing apparel as dinner togs in your dunnage, as you call it?"

"Dinner togs?" echoed Mackeller, aghast. "Why, hang it all, I'm a mining engineer. I haven't even a starched shirt with me, let alone a dress suit. I didn't know I was coming to an evening party?"

"No, you paid attention to the trivialities of life, such as rifles and ammunition, and quite neglected the more important affair of costume."

"I'll eat forward with the men," said Mackeller gruffly.

"Oh, there's no need for that. As you tried to bolt through the door from my breakfast room the other day, when Ponderby was on guard, I saw him measure your proportions critically with his eye, in case it should be necessary for him to use that force which I deplore, so I told Ponderby to make a guess at what would fit you, and to go to the extent of three evening suits of varying sizes made to order. You will find them all laid out in your room, and the able Ponderby will give you critical advice regarding which fits you best."

"Well, sir, if you expect me to look pretty every night— —"

"Oh, no," interrupted his lordship, "I never expect the impossible, but, you see, Captain Wilkie is rather a stickler on etiquette. He will occupy one end of the table, brave in a uniform of gold lace made by the premier naval tailor of London, so we must play up to him, my boy, and do the best we can. Then there will be our chief engineer, also in uniform, and the wireless telegraphy operator, who is rather a la-de-da young man, and lastly there's the doctor, an Oxford graduate, and so we must do honor to the university. You and I are in the minority, and we'll just need to make the best of it."

Mackeller departed dejectedly to his room, which he found so spacious and so luxuriously fitted up that he stood on its threshold for a few moments, dumfounded, regarding it with dismay. He emerged when the gong rang, and entered the long broad saloon which extended from side to side of the ship. Lord Stranleigh occupied the head of the table, and he introduced Mackeller to Dr. Holden, and to Mr. Spencer, electrician and telegrapher. Neither the captain nor the engineer put in an appearance during dinner, the one waiting to see his ship in more open waters, and the other standing by to watch the behavior of the machinery at the beginning of a long run.

"You have a fine boat here, Stranleigh," said the doctor.

"It isn't half bad," admitted his lordship. "Still, there's always a fly in the ointment. I call her *The Woman in White*, after the title of Wilkie Collins's famous novel. You know the book, Mac-keller, I suppose?"

"I never heard of it. I don't read novels."

"Oh, well, we must convert you before the voyage is ended. You'll find plenty of fiction on board this boat. There's a copy of "The Woman in White" in every room, large and small, each copy in a style of binding that suits the decoration of the room, so I beg of you, Mackeller, to begin reading the story in your own apartment, and if, getting interested in it, you wish to continue in the saloon, or on deck, I hope you will take the saloon or deck copy, so that the color of the binding will not clash with your surroundings. I ought really to have the copies chained in their places, as was the case with the ancient books in our churches, for it is a terribly distressing sight to see a man reading a mauve book in a white-and-gold saloon, or a scarlet copy up on deck."

"Yes, I should think that would be appalling," sneered Mackeller.

"Now, don't be sarcastic, Peter, and thus lacerate my tenderest artistic tastes. You may come to know, some day, when you are starving in a wilderness on the West Coast, that these are really the serious things of life."

"I dare say," replied Peter gruffly.

"Then the fly in the ointment," said the doctor, "is the fact that your passengers persist in taking away the volumes from the rooms where they belong?"

"Oh, no; a man who calls his yacht *Woman in White*, should have a captain named Wilkie Collins. I searched England and Scotland for one of that name, and couldn't find him, so I was compelled to compromise, a thing I always dislike doing. My captain's name is Wilkie, and my chief engineer's name is Collins, and thus I divide the burden of congruity upon the shoulders of two different men, whereas one would have sufficed if his parents had only exhibited some common sense at his christening. I'd pay any salary in reason for a captain named Wilkie Collins."

"I think I'll write a book myself, some day," said the doctor, "and call it 'The Grievous Worries of a Millionaire.' Would you object if I took you as my model for my Croesus?"

"On the contrary, I should be flattered, and as you progress with the work I may be able to supply you with incidents to weave into your narrative."

Mackeller sat silent while this frivolous conversation went on, and this silence he maintained during the greater part of the voyage. Mackeller's mind was troubled. He was a serious young man, whose opinions were strongly grounded on common sense, and there were many elements in the situation that gave him just cause for anxiety. When it came down to finalities, he possessed a strong belief in the efficiency of force. So far as his knowledge went, the Lord was always on the side of the biggest battalion. He represented the American confidence in the big stick, the British faith in keeping your powder dry, the German reliance on the mailed fist.

And now here he was treading the deck of a confection in naval construction; a dainty flower of marine architecture, which slipped through the water as gracefully as if she were a living white swan. Her well-molded, snowy sides were of the finest quality of pressed steel, almost paper thin, and he was convinced that even a single shot from a small cannon would send her shivering to the bottom, shattering her metal covering as a pane of glass is shattered by a well-thrown stone, and for this delusion he was scarcely to be blamed, because his education had been concentrated on mining engineering, and the mechanism of air-tight and water-tight compartments did not form part of his curriculum. He knew that on the open sea *The Woman in White* could not be overtaken by any craft afloat except one or other of the most recent torpedo-boat destroyers, which were not likely to be encountered along the west coast of Africa, but he knew the locality to which *The Woman in White* was bound, and he pictured her from twelve to twenty-four miles away from the coast, where, if discovered, she would need to make her way down a narrow river, flanked on each side, after she left the shelter of the hills, by a flat country. In this position it would be impossible, owing to windings of the stream, to take advantage of her full speed, and being under the misapprehension that a single well-aimed shot would disable, if not sink, her, he pictured the beautiful yacht and her crew helplessly trapped somewhere between the hills and the lagoon, at the mercy of well-armed, desperate men, in a region where no law, save that of might, ran: men who would not feel the slightest scruple in removing from the earth, all trace of the vessel and those aboard of her.

If Mackeller had been told that the little craft might have been riddled like a sieve, and still keep afloat, and that so long as a stray shot did not destroy her motive power, she could, within a few minutes, get out of range of any land force, so long as there was a sufficient depth of water in the river, he would not have believed it. He strongly suspected that the *Rajah* was well provided not only with cannon and ammunition, but also with floating mines to seal up the river, rendering exit impossible. Into this fatal *impasse* Lord Stranleigh, with a levity that saddened Mackeller, was running his unprotected cruiser, armed only with luxury. Officers and crew would be of little use in a fight, and the extra men, whatever might be the shooting qualities of the gamekeepers and foresters whom Stranleigh had requisitioned from his estates, were quite undisciplined, and although most of them were doubtless expert enough with a shotgun, their efficiency with magazined arms of precision such as he had sent on board, was more than doubtful.

Once or twice during the early portion of the voyage, Mackeller had endeavored to imbue Lord Stranleigh with some of his own apprehension, but the young nobleman was usually in company with the doctor, or with the telegrapher, or one or other of the officers, and he invariably turned aside Mackeller's attempts with a joke, refusing to discuss anything seriously. By the time they had arrived at that portion of the waters where they should have passed the *Rajah,* according to Mackeller's calculation, they were sailing through an empty sea. Day after day Mackeller, from the front of the vessel, swept the bald horizon with the most powerful of binoculars, but he saw nothing of the tramp steamer. The voyage had been monotonous with its good weather. Nothing had happened, either in the way of a breakdown of machinery, or the encountering of even a moderate storm.

Lord Stranleigh recognized his anxious search with an amused smile, but said nothing. At last Mackeller gave up scrutiny of sea and sky. It was no longer possible that the *Rajah* could have covered the distance *The Woman in White* had already traversed. Still, his earnest meditations had at last evolved a plan, and the adoption of that plan he must now urge upon his chief, so seeing that Stranleigh, for once, was alone, he strode aft to the spot where the head of the expedition lolled in a reclining cane chair, with his slippered feet extended on the adjustable rest. Like the woman for whom his ship was named, he was clad entirely in white, for the weather was warm, although the yacht slipped so speedily through the oily water that a comforting breeze greeted every one on deck. The young man placed the book he had been reading face downward on the little table at his elbow, and looked up at the on-comer with an expression of amusement on his face.

"Well, Mackeller," he cried, "have you found her?"

"Found whom, sir?"

"Why, the *Rajah,* of course."

"How did you know I was looking for her?"

"You've been looking for something these few days past, so I took the liberty of surmising it was the *Rajah.*"

"You are quite right.'"

"I always am, Mackeller. Haven't you discovered that yet? Always be right and then you'll be happy, although you'll also be extremely disliked by everybody else. Still, I never aimed at popularity, not wishing to write a book, or stand for Parliament, so a lack of popularity does not matter."

"I never pretend to be always right, sir."

"Well, that's a good thing. I dislike pretense myself; nevertheless, it is so easy to be right that I sometimes wonder you don't practice the art. All that is necessary is knowledge and brains."

"I do not lack knowledge in my own line of business, and no one ever hinted before that I was lacking in brain power."

"I do not hint that at all, Mackeller. I bear willing testimony to your brain power, but I sometimes think you don't exercise it enough. For instance, you think things out in somber silence, when sometimes a question might throw a good deal of light on your problem. Take my own actions, for instance. Do you suppose I wish the whereabouts of my yacht reported in the marine columns of the English newspapers day by day, thus running the risk that certain people will begin to wonder what I am doing so far south?"

"Of course not."

"Very well. Why have we met none of the South African liners, or overtaken any of the tramps threshing their way to Cape Town?"

"I'm sure I don't know."

"Oh, yes, you do, if you'll only think. The reason is this: that having ample time at my command, the course of my yacht was deflected from south to southwest when we reached north latitude 40. We spun along merrily in that direction till daylight did appear, and then resumed our progress south. We passed outside of the islands, and out of the track of any steamer that might report us. Now turn your brain power upon that amiable gentleman who kicked you downstairs. He must at least strongly suspect that he's engaged on an illegal expedition. Would he deflect, do you think, and waste valuable time on the face of the ocean?"

"No, I don't think so."

"Of course you don't. He'd make for your what-do-you-call-it river on a bee-line. The course we have taken puts us two hundred miles, more or less, from his path, and as they tell me you cannot see more than thirty miles on the water, you may now conjecture how fruitless has been your scanning of the ocean. I had no desire to see the *Rajah*, but in any case I did not wish the *Rajah* to see me. We will steam as we are going until we are directly opposite your gold mine; then round at right angles and straight eastward is our course. You should do as I do, Mackeller, and read that incomparable sea writer, W. Clark Russell, then you'd begin to understand what you are about. He'd put you up to all the tricks of the trade. It's one of his books I'm perusing now, which accounts for my trickiness at sea. Have you ever read any of his novels?"

"No, I haven't."

"Very well, then, begin with the 'Wreck of the Grosvenor.' We've got all his works on board, and pretty soon you'll know what to do with a mutiny, how to conduct yourself when marooned, the proper etiquette to adopt if tackled by a cyclone, what to say when you and a nice girl are left alone on a wreck. Of course I admit that W. W. Jacobs is excellent, and that he puts forth most admirable text-books on navigation, but he is only good below-bridge, as you might put it; for rivers and other inland waters, and perhaps a bit of the coast. When you take to deep-sea navigation you must study Clark Russell, my boy. Take the advice of a tarry old salt like myself, and study Clark Russell. Do not be deluded by my white apparel; I am tar to the finger ends, and full of salt junk, because I'm three quarter way through his latest book."

"I suppose it would be useless for me to say, sir, that I believe you are running into a trap?"

"Oh, quite. Sufficient to the day is the evil thereof. You refer, of course, to our being bottled up in that unpronounceable river, and ordinarily I should give some attention to the matter, but I cannot now, as I am in the middle of the most exciting chapter in this most exciting book. Once we are inside the trap, Mackeller, we'll study its construction, and find a way out. There seems to me little practical use in studying an imaginary trap which may not be there when we arrive. That leads to disappointment. Let us first get into the trap if we can; then if there's no way out, we will console ourselves by the knowledge that there are plenty of provisions and books to read on board. If the worst comes to the worst, we will get our wireless telegraphy at work until we pick up a liner similarly equipped, and thus get into communication with Clark Russell, relate our position, and ask him what to do. I'll bet you a fiver he'll send a solution of the problem."

Mackeller compressed his lips, and turned on his heel without a word.

"Oh, very well," laughed Stranleigh, "have it your own way. Try Jacobs if you like, but I bank on Russell," and with that parting remark his lordship resumed his reading.

Mackeller grimly resolved to make no further attempt to instill common sense into an empty head, neither did he take to the reading of freshwater or salt-water authors. He devoted what time remained to him in poring over certain scientific works he had discovered in the library.

One night he woke up suddenly. The boat was strangely still. Light as had been the unceasing purr of the turbines, its cessation had instantly aroused him. He made his way to the deck. The steamer swayed gently in the heave of the sea. From the east came the low murmur of breakers on the shore, sounding like a distant waterfall. The dim outline of dark hills against a less dark sky could be distinguished, and that was all. Mackeller paced the deck until daylight, when the steamer got under weigh again, and cautiously approached the shore. One of the ship's boats was swung into the water, and under Mackeller's guidance sounded with a lead the depths of the channel, the yacht crawling after them, until at last it entered the river. By nine o'clock it was moored alongside the gold fields. A few minutes later Lord Stranleigh appeared on deck, well-groomed, clear-eyed, and fresh as a youth whose night's rest has been undisturbed. He expressed no surprise on seeing the position of his steamer, but merely remarked to his captain:

"That was rather a good shot, old man, considering the size of the target and the distance. When did you sight the coast?"

"At four bells, sir."

"Did you need to cruise up and down to find the spot?"

"No, sir."

"Look at that, now, and yet Maekeller thinks we're going to be trapped."

After breakfast Lord Stranleigh gave orders that the steamer should proceed upstream to the head of navigation, wherever that was, so they cast off, and began to explore. They discovered that the stream they were navigating was merely a branch, and not the main river, as Mackeller had supposed. About a mile above the mines the land began to rise, and both banks were clothed with splendid forests. Arriving at the head of the delta they found that the river itself proceeded due north, while a branch similar to that which passed the gold fields struck off through the forest to the southwest. The southwest branch was the smallest of the three streams, so they did not trouble with it, but went down the main river until they reached a defile with hills to the west of them facing the continuous range to the east.

"This will be our camping spot, I imagine," said Stranleigh. "We will return to it, but first I wish to investigate the channel at the mouth of the river."

They discovered, to Mackeller's surprise, that the stream flowed so far to the north that when at last it turned west the steamer could reach the ocean without any possibility of being seen from the gold region. Stranleigh laughed when this fact was made plain, and smote Mackeller on the shoulders.

"Where's your trap now, my boy?" he cried. "You would have saved yourself some worry if you had known that the lay of the land was like this."

"Nevertheless," said Mackeller, "if they discover this channel, they may fill it with floating mines:"

"So they may the mouth of the Thames, but they won't. An engineer should stick to probabilities, Peter. Now we will return, and seek our secluded glen, mooring against the eastern bank, so that if we are discovered by our opponents, as the song says, they will have one more river to cross."

They reached the ravine in the evening, and Lord Stranleigh complained of a hard day's work virtuously accomplished, with the prospective dinner well earned, although his exertions had consisted mainly of sitting in an armchair at the prow, with his feet on the rail.

Next morning he crossed the river with Mackeller and a party of foresters, some of whom carried axes, one a huge telescope with its stand, and another a small tent. At the top the foresters cleared away intervening underbrush so that a view might be had of the distant gold fields. The telescope stand was placed upon the rock, and the tent erected over it. Stranleigh, adjusting the focus, gazed at the gold fields, then rubbed his hands with satisfaction.

"Why," he said, "we can see their inmost thoughts with this."

When they descended, Stranleigh sent another party to the top, one laden with wireless telegraphy apparatus, which the operator was requested to get into working order.

"If successful it will save us a telephone wire," said his lordship.

The rest were laden with provisions.

"Mackeller," he said, "I appoint you to the outlook, and your companion will be our second telegraph operator. One never knows what may happen in this locality, so if our steamer is compelled to cut and run, you people up on top, with everything so well concealed, can lie low, yet keep in touch with us so long as we are within the four-mile radius, or whatever is the limit of the wireless. I noticed a little spring about halfway up in the forest, and that will supply you with drink nearer than the river, and I counsel you it is better for you than champagne, although I have sent up a ease of that. And now, to show you how economical I am, and thus make an appeal to your Scottish heart, I am going to send my woodmen into the forest alongside, and while here we will burn nothing but hard wood, and save coal. Indeed, I have consulted with my chief engineer, and with his consent I am going to fill our bunkers with the most combustible timber I can find. I take no further interest in your mountain top until the *Rajah* is sighted, but while the woodmen, with their axes and saws, are filling the bunkers, I shall attend to the larder with fishing tackle and gun, and here's where my gamekeepers will earn their wages."

Game proved to be plentiful, and many wondrous fishes were captured.

"Oh!" cried Stranleigh, one night after an exceptionally good fish and game dinner. "Piccadilly is a fool of a place to this. If the postal arrangements were only a little better, we would be all right. I must send a letter to the *Times* about the negligence of our Government, and score the postmaster-general, as all right-minded correspondents do. I have almost forgotten what a postman looks like, but I expect when we get our wireless at work we'll be able to give Signor Marconi some hints when we return."

The *Rajah* was three days late, according to Mackeller's calculations, but one morning Mac-keller recognized her slowly stemming the current of the Paramakaboo River, and at once the information was telegraphed to Stranleigh, who did not receive the message, as he was out shooting. The young man had taken his lunch with him, so the operator on the steamer informed those up aloft, and no one knew when he would be back.

Mackeller, his eye glued to the telescope, watched the landing of the army that the Rajah carried, and saw the two steam cranes, one fore and one aft, begin at once to swing ashore the cargo from the hold. He momentarily expected the arrival of his chief, but the dinner hour came, bringing no visitor to the hilltop. Mackeller and the operator descended, and there, to his amazement, on the after-deck he saw Stranleigh seated, calmly reading a novel, and awaiting the sound of the gong.

"Didn't you get our message?" demanded Mackeller.

"Oh, yes, a couple of hours ago. The *Rajah* has come in, you say? That's very interesting. You'll be glad to know, Mackeller, that I have had a most successful day's shooting."

"Yes, that, as you remark, is very interesting," replied Mackeller dryly. "I thought, if you got my message in time, you would have come up to the outlook."

"I am sorry to have disappointed you, Peter, but when I place an excellent man on the spot I never interfere with him. I should be quite superfluous on the hilltop, and it's so much more comfortable down here."

"You might have been surprised to know how many men they landed from the *Rajah*. Enough, I estimate, to clean us up in short order if they find us."

"Well, let us hope they won't find us, Peter."

"They've got a number of tents erected already, and they began blasting operations at one o'clock."

"They are not losing any time, are they?"

"No, they are not. I see they have arranged electric searchlights on the two masts, apparently to cover the field of operations, so I suppose they will be working day and night shifts."

"I do love an energetic body of men," said his lordship with admiration. "If there was a funicular to the top of your hill, I'd take up an armchair merely for the pleasure of sitting and watching them. Ah, there's the dinner gong, thank goodness. Peter, I shot some birds to-day that I think you'll enjoy."

"Thank you, but all I wish is a sandwich. I'm going back to the outlook. We haven't broken into the boxes of provisions yet. I must learn if these people are actually going to work all night."

"Take my advice, Peter, and don't. Enjoy a good rest in your comfortable bed. Those who sleep well live long."

"I am going back," said Peter.

"Ah, I see what you're trying to do. You'll force me to give you both a day and a night salary, or perhaps you are yearning to imitate the energy of those johnnies on the gold rock. Now do be persuaded, for my sake, to consume a good dinner when it is all ready for you. Place the sandwiches in your pocket, if you like, to munch during the watches of the night, if you will persist in climbing that distressingly steep hill."

Mackeller shook his head.

"I implore you to be persuaded, Peter, because if you will not succumb to gentle measures, I shall command you, and then if you refuse, I'll put you in irons. I'm not going to tramp all day over Africa on your behalf, and then have my bag ignored when I return. One concession I will make: don't trouble to-night about your evening clothes. Be not abashed by the splendor of your table companions, but devote your attention to the dinner, which I hope you will pronounce good, and I will order the steward to make you up a parcel of delicious sandwiches."

So Mackeller, being a hired minion, was forced to comply. At the head of the table that evening, Lord Stranleigh held forth eloquently on the wickedness of work.

"I don't agree with my friend, President Roosevelt," he said, "regarding the strenuous life. The President quite overlooks the fact that work was placed upon this earth as a curse, and now many unthinking people pretend to look upon it as a blessing. Roosevelt reminds me something of Mackeller here, except that he is more genial, and possesses a greater sense of humor. Mackeller, actuated by the promptings of duty, and assisted by porridge-fed muscle, is actually going to climb that steeple of a hill tonight, while we will be playing bridge. This will give him a feeling of superiority over us which to-morrow he will be unable to conceal. I always sympathize with those people who eliminated Aristides called the Just."

Mackeller remained silent through all this badinage, but nevertheless enjoyed his dinner, although the moment coffee was served and the card table set out, he rowed himself across the river, tied up his boat securely, and ascended through the darkness of the forest to see the electric lights blazing over the gold mine when he reached the top.

In spite of his apparent indifference, Lord Stranleigh appeared on the summit shortly after breakfast. He found Mackeller stretched on the rock, sound asleep, and did not disturb him, but turned his attention instead to the telescope, through which he saw enough of industry going on to satisfy the most indolent. He turned the telescope this way and that, and at last fixed it at a point covering the river lower down than the mine. There he gazed quietly for a long time, until interrupted by Mackeller sitting up, and giving utterance to an exclamation when he saw his chief seated on the stump that did duty for a chair.

"Good morning, Peter. Watchman, what of the night?"

"They worked all night, sir, both at the blasting of the ore, and the unloading of the ship."

"Then that means we shall soon need to be getting under weigh again. If they load the *Rajah* as quickly as they have unloaded her, she will be out in the ocean before we know where we are."

"That's why I came up last night, sir. I thought you didn't quite appreciate how speedily our visit here is drawing to a close."

"And yet," drawled Stranleigh, "what they are doing now seems to point to a lengthened stay on the part of the *Rajah*."

"What are they doing now?" demanded Mackeller.

"About half a mile below the gold fields they are planting floating mines in the river. They have just finished one row that goes clear across the stream, and are engaged upon the second series a quarter of a mile, as I estimate the distance, nearer the ocean. They have two ordinary ship's boats at work, and one steam launch. The river is sealed up, and there is a practical declaration of war, my boy, with Mackeller sound asleep."

CHAPTER V—AN INVITATION TO LUNCH

MACKELLER, now wide awake, sprang to his feet and gazed through the telescope. "You see," he cried triumphantly, "I was right after all!"

"Yes, you were right on one point and wrong on another. I confess I did not believe in the floating mine, because it is not an article you can buy at every ironmonger's; but you were wrong in predicting they would leave a channel for the *Rajah* to get out: they have completely sealed the river. Of course that is an advantage. When it is time for the *Rajah* to leave, you will see those mines picked up and brought inshore; so, by watching the mine field on the river, we will receive notice of the *Rajah's* departure."

"And do you intend to follow her out when the mines are cleared away?"

"Bless you, no. We will depart by the main channel."

"Then you will do nothing about this nest of explosives?"

"What is there to do? If we were Japanese, and reckless of human life, we might steal down there and set the mines adrift; but that would be a dangerous business, and if one or more got out into the ocean we might find ourselves practically responsible for the destruction of a Cape liner. But after all," continued his lordship dreamily, sprawling at full length on the place that Mackeller had deserted, "after all, what is the use of this gold? You can't eat it or drink it, except in London or Paris, or some such center of so-called civilization. You have just seen what brutes it makes of men in quest of it, when they will in cold blood prepare for the annihilation of their fellow creatures."

"But you knew all that, sir, before you left England."

"True, true, so I did; but here the fact has made a greater impression on my mind. I have arrived at a theory. I believe this spot to be the Garden of Eden. The soil and climate will grow anything. You may enjoy whatever temperature you like by simply rising higher and higher in the hills; the higher you get the lower the temperature.

There is ample timber of all kinds, and yesterday I discovered a lovely waterfall which would give us enough electricity to endow a city with power, so I intend to found a modern Utopia, and have selected a spot where this very day we will begin to clear away the forest and build log huts. The nucleus of our colony will be situated at the head of the delta alongside the stream that passes the gold field and flows direct to the ocean. I shall move the steamer over there, and thus, Peter, you will be deserted, for I insist that you shall watch our potential enemies from this spot, and report by wireless what they are doing."

"So you intend to give up this mining property without a struggle?"

"Oh, I hate struggling. The climate is too perfect to struggle. Let us be happy when there is a chance of happiness."

The young man reclined there with his hands clasped behind his head, looking up quizzically with half-closed eyes at the bewildered Mackeller.

"By the way, Mackeller, there is something afloat on the river near the yacht that would interest you. Did I tell you I had picked up a little gem of a motor boat at Thomycroft's, actually armored and bullet-proof? In it we could go down and visit the mine, and return, letting them pepper away at us, while we lay full length on deck protected by the armored bulwarks. No one could be hit, unless the shooter were on top of a church steeple. I think I'll visit the mining camp."

"I strongly advise you, sir, to do nothing of the kind."

"Oh, very well, I won't, then, but this little craft will come in handy for visiting you. It is a nimble little beast, and much more effective on these waters than the row boat."

"Are you in earnest about that Utopia, sir?"

"Certainly, which reminds me I must make a beginning."

He rose, lazily stretched himself, nodded good-by to Mackeller, and proceeded in leisurely fashion down the hill.

The woodmen on board *The Woman in White* received the announcement of the new Utopia in a spirit quite differing from that of Mackeller, but of course they knew nothing of the gold that had been the object of the cruise. The yacht proceeded to the side of the plateau that Stranleigh had selected as the site of his first village, and presently the air was filled with a crash of falling trees, with the ringing sound of the ax, and the snarl of the saw. Gamekeepers and crew were all set to work, those who could not chop being useful at the two-handed saw, or the rolling of logs to the river bank, where Stranleigh ordered them to be piled.

Mackeller and the telegrapher occupied their lonely perch night and day, and sent in reports of progress. At last Mackeller announced that the loading of ore had gone so far that the Plim-soll's mark on the *Rajah's* side was already submerged, which fact, added Mackeller, showed that the steamer did not intend sailing to England. Within half an hour of the receipt of this message the swift little motor boat brought Stran-leigh and the doctor to the foot of Outlook Hill, and presently the two arrived at the summit.

"Mackeller," said Stranleigh, "turn your telescope upstream to the first bit of clear water you see."

While Mackeller was doing this, the chief turned to the operator—and said:

"Send a message to your colleague: these words—'Let'em all come.' Ask him to repeat them to show that he has understood."

"Are you expecting an attack?" asked Mackeller, putting his own interpretation on the familiar defiant phrase.

"A sort of an attack," replied Stranleigh. "You watch the surface of that water, and tell me what you see."

"Oh!" cried Mackeller, "there seems to be a raft coming down."

"No, they are separate logs. They have understood our signal, doctor, and have acted promptly. Now, Mackeller, turn your glass on the floating mines, and give up your place to the doctor. I have promised him the first sight. How many mines did they lay down, Mackeller?"

"I don't know, sir."

"Ah, yes, I remember; you were asleep at your post. Well, I'm happy to inform you that the number I saw placed in the river was exactly twenty-seven. Now, Mr. Telegrapher, stand up here and make yourself useful. If explosions occur, no man is to speak, but each is to keep count of the number of spurts of water he sees, then we will compare notes at the end of the fusillade."

"By Jove!" exclaimed the doctor, his eyes glued to the telescope.

A tall pillar of water, white as snow, rose into the air, paused, broke like a sky-rocket, and subsided in a misty rain, which the wind caught and blew along the surface of the water. Then three more shot up into the air as if in competition. A sound like distant thunder came across the delta, and now it seemed that one mine had set off another, or else the logs were even thicker than might have been expected, for a wall of water rose from the surface of the river, extending, with breaks here and there, from shore to shore, and instead of a rumble, a sharp thunderclap was heard by the four men on the mountain. This made counting impossible. For a few moments nothing further happened, then a quarter of a mile down the river the line of mines went off practically simultaneously, forming for a brief instant a Niagara in the sky.

"I think we've got them," said Stranleigh quietly, as he slung over his shoulder again the binoculars he had been using. "Turn your telescope to the land again, doctor, and see those comical people tumbling over each other in their haste to find out what has happened. They look like a nest of disturbed ants."

"What have you done with the yacht?" asked Mackeller. "If any of those people have seen sawn logs float down the river there will be an investigation very speedily to discover who has done the sawing."

"That is true, Mackeller. I have therefore taken the yacht across the river out of gunshot, or the sight of our abandoned Utopia. If they come by land they can't reach her."

"They are not coming by land," said the doctor. "The steam launch is being got ready, and three men are standing on the rock ledge preparing to go aboard, I fancy. They are armed with rifles, too."

"Just glance through the telescope, Mackeller," said Stranleigh, "and tell me if you recognize the three men."

"Yes; there is the tall manager, with the captain of the *Rajah* on one side of him, and the first mate on the other."

"Don't say 'first mate,' Peter," corrected Stranleigh. "Clark Russell says there's no such thing as a first mate. He is merely the mate, and then you have second and third mate, and I don't know how many more. Well, doctor, let us get away, and meet them in the motor boat. We're innocent lumbermen, searching for timber that has tumbled off the bank, remember."

"You are surely not going down there," protested Mackeller.

"Why, of course. We'll fill them up with our story before they even begin to ask questions."

"But you are unarmed."

"Quite."

"And they possess rifles."

"So it seems."

"Then it is a foolhardy thing to meet them without being accompanied by an equal body of armed men to protect you, at least. I should take all that the motor boat will hold."

"I know you would, Peter, but then, as I have often said, you are a bloodthirsty person. We can drop behind the bulwarks flat on our faces, before any one of the three can shoot; then in that recumbent position I will explain to them as well as I can that the Thornycroft motor boat possesses a submarine prow as effective as that of a battle ship, and if they don't want their steam launch rammed and sunk, they'd better drop their rifles to the deck. I shall insist that whoever speaks to me shall talk as one gentleman to another. I'll tell them I'm a member of the Peace Conference at The Hague. Come along, doctor. We'll invite those johnnies to lunch, and cheer them up with the best wine and cigars that's to be had in Africa," and with that Stranleigh and the doctor departed for the waiting motor boat.

The steersman of the little motor boat crouched over his wheel, which had some resemblance to that of an automobile, as the swift craft sped up the river until it came to the branch that led to the mine, then into this watery lane it turned at full speed. Stranleigh and the doctor were standing up, and on rounding a bend came in sight of the steam launch laboriously churning up toward them against the current.

"Stop the engine," said Stranleigh. "Swing round the stem of the launch, and come up alongside at a distance of about twenty feet, then regulate her speed to suit that of the launch."

The manager, captain, and mate, all standing up, seemed struck into immobility with astonishment at seeing such a cutter in such a region.

They made no motion to raise their guns, or even to salute the oncomer. The motor boat came past them like a wild duck, without sound of machinery or sight of vapor, swung gracefully round, and came up alongside with a light precision which should have aroused the admiration of an old salt like the captain of the *Rajah*.

But the three men were filled with consternation. The ruddy, weather-beaten face of the captain turned to a mottled purple; his jaw dropped, and he stood there gaping, with fear in his bulging eyes. The erect, easy grace of Lord Stran-leigh, clad in white, instantly suggested to his experienced eye the British naval officer. This error was heightened by the natty, gold-braided hat worn by the doctor; but the attitude of the two men in white was not so disquieting as the demeanor and appearance of the boat herself. She was most expertly handled, and came alongside with that impudent, saucy air characteristic of midshipmen and the smaller units of the British navy. There was a touch of arrogance in her rakish build, as if she knew the whole power of a maritime nation was typified in her. The significance of her armored sides was not lost on the two seafaring men, even though the manager of the mine did not become immediately conscious of it, but all three recognized the sinister significance of that projecting prow of steel, which was plainly, if waveringly seen, through the transparent green waters, dangerous as the nose of a maneating shark.

Lord Stranleigh smiled as he realized the panic his sudden appearance had caused.

"The three men were filled with consternation."

"Good morning," he greeted them pleasantly. "Have you seen anything of timber floating down this river?"

"Timber?" gasped the manager of the mine. "Yes—yes—we have."

"Is it lost, do you think?"

"I—I suppose most of it is bobbing about in the surf of the Atlantic Ocean."

"Not lost, but gone before," murmured the doctor.

Stranleigh surmised that captain and mate knew more of the piratical, thieving nature of their expedition than he had supposed.

They were both well aware that British cruisers were nosing about in all sorts of odd comers of the world, mostly where they were not wanted, but even so a worthy seaman, if engaged in his lawful occupation, had no reason to fall into a state of nervous collapse at the sight of a craft which looked like a baby torpedo boat. He had hitherto believed that captain, officers, and crew of the *Rajah* were innocent participators in a scheme of villainy and theft, but now he knew that the captain and mate were equally in the plot with the tall, dark-looking manager, and this information he placed at the back of his brain for future use when he should meet the captain on the open sea.

"Are you a naval officer, sir?" stammered the captain, speaking for the first time.

"Oh, dear, no," replied Stranleigh airily; "merely a private person."

All three heaved a simultaneous sigh of relief, and their statuesque posture lost something of its stiffness.

"I'm cruising about the coast in my yacht."

"That isn't your yacht, is it?" asked the mine manager.

"No, my yacht lies a few miles farther up the river, and is an ocean-going affair. It is built with an eye to comfort and to the housing of a good number of men."

"Ah, how many men do you carry?" demanded the manager, his courage visibly returning.

"Blessed if I know," replied his lordship. "How many men have we, doctor?"

"I never counted them, sir," replied the doctor with a noncommittal air of indifference.

"They are scattered over the face of the country," continued the chief. "Many of them are woodmen, and the rest are gamekeepers from my own estates in England. They can all shoot a bit—trust a gamekeeper for that."

"And is your yacht built on the model of this boat of yours?"

"No. As I told you, it is built for comfort. I'd like very much to show her to you if you will honor me with a visit. Indeed, it is getting near to midday, so I should be delighted if you three gentlemen would be good enough to lunch with me. I can promise you a passable meal, some excellent wine, and cigars that will call up recollections of Havana."

The manager whispered to the captain, who somewhat doubtfully nodded his head, as who would say: "Well, I suppose we'd better see what's in this, anyway."

The manager then spoke up:

"Thank you, sir," he said. "We'll be very glad of a bite and a drink and a smoke. My friend here is captain of the *Rajah*, and this is Mr. Thompson, the mate. I am Frowningshield, representing the owners of this district."

"Delighted to make your acquaintance, gentlemen. My name is Stranleigh."

"And a very well-known name in Africa, Mr. Stanley."

"S-t-r-a-n-l-e-i-g-h," spelled his lordship. "I cannot claim the distinction of being a namesake of the explorer."

"May I inquire the object of your visit in these regions?" asked the manager.

"In a small way I am looking after big game, and so carry some of my gamekeepers with me. Then again, as you are probably aware, I am interested in timber, hence my woodmen with their axes and saws. We have cut a considerable quantity of firewood, with which we hope to supplement our coal. My third object may strike you as largely impractical. I had some thoughts of founding a settlement here, or on any other healthy and suitable spot not too far from the coast. I am delighted with this section of the country. Back in the hills while shooting I have discovered several waterfalls which could supply cheap power. Some days ago I gave orders to my woodmen to prepare logs for the building of huts. I was away shooting at the time they began operations, and I fear rather neglecting my duties as a settlement founder. Be that as it may, they piled the logs too near the brink of the river, where the incline is steep. This morning, like the Gadarene swine, the logs seem to have tumbled one after another into the water. I suppose one heap set another going. As I tell you, I was absent, but when word was brought to me, I took this launch and followed down the river, thinking perhaps the sawn logs had lodged or jammed somewhere, and might be towed back; but if, as you say, they are already in the ocean, I fear they are lost to us, and we'll need to cut some more."

Frowningshield listened to this recital with wrinkled brow, and intense gaze upon the speaker, who talked in an easy, indolent manner which impressed the manager with the belief that he had encountered some rich fool with more money at his disposal than was good for him, and gradually the nerve of the man who had kicked Mackeller into the hold began to reassert itself. He felt ashamed of his failure in courage when he had supposed he was confronted by the power of Great Britain.

"Perhaps you are not aware, Mr. Stranleigh, that the timber you are cutting is situated on private property."

"You are surely mistaken," protested the young man. "All the maps I have seen—I'll show you them when we come aboard the yacht—depict this district as a sort of no-man's-land."

"Such is not the case, Mr. Stranleigh. More than a hundred square miles of this territory has been acquired by a European syndicate, of whom I am the representative."

"You amaze me. From what government did this syndicate buy the property?"

"They did not buy it from any government, they acquired the concession from native chiefs. No European government holds jurisdiction over this section of Africa."

"That's what I thought. Are you forming a settlement, then, farther down the river? Is that where you have come from?"

"Yes."

"You arrived in the steamer you spoke of—I forget the name?"

"The *Rajah*. Yes. I am a mining engineer, and we are experimenting with the mineral resources of this country."

"I see. Then you are probably loading the *Rajah* with such ore as you can find, and are taking it back to Europe to test it."

"Exactly."

"What you tell me is most interesting, but surely you were not here when I came up this river in my yacht less than a month ago?"

"No, we were not here then, but we prospected, and secured possession more than a year ago."

"Then you are clothed with authority to order me to move on?"

"I assure you, Mr. Stranleigh, that so far as I am personally concerned you might form your settlement, or stay here as long as you please, but I am not acting for myself. In the interest of my employers, and to prevent future complications, should we discover valuable minerals, I fear I must warn you off."

"Could you oblige me with the address of that European syndicate?"

"It would be useless, sir. I was instructed that they do not intend to grant any concessions or franchises to outsiders. Whether they gain or lose, they intend to exploit this region for their own sole benefit. If you dispute my authority, I shall be pleased to produce documentary evidence corroborating what I say."

"My dear Mr. Frowningshield," protested Stranleigh, "I should not dream of disputing your authority. I confess I was rather taken with this upper country, though I don't think much of the stretch of land along the coast. However, Africa is large, and I do not doubt I may find some spot equally favorable for the carrying out of my plans. What you say merely shows how small the world is getting to be. Who would have imagined that in this seemingly virgin territory, thousands of miles from what we call civilization, the land should be all taken up, just as if it were a newly plotted piece of acreage in the vicinity of New York or London, to be exploited and covered with jerry-built villas. Well, well, we live and learn. It's rather disappointing, but it can't be helped. I hope you won't send in an exorbitant bill for the trees I have illegally felled, especially when you remember that I have lost most of the timber."

"Oh, no," said Frowningshield, with a laugh. "That will be all right."

"It seems so strange that I, of all people, should be a trespasser and a poacher, for when at home I am a stern upholder of the rights of property. I own several estates in England, and am a very pig-headed Tory when any of my privileges are threatened; so I should be the last man to trespass on the rights of others, and I hope, Mr. Frowningshield, when you are communicating with the proprietors, you will convey to them my humble apologies, with the assurance that if ever again I fell a tree, I shall take pains to know it has grown on my own land."

"Oh, that will be all right," repeated Frowningshield reassuringly.

"There!" cried Stranleigh, as they approached the triple outflow, and waving his hand to the right, "you see the gash I have made in your forest. That is the spot I had chosen for the nucleus of my settlement. There are the remainder of the logs, and I present them freely to you with no charge for the cutting."

"They are piled rather close to the edge," commented Frowningshield.

"Yes, we all realize that now, when it is too late. Locking the door when the horse is stolen. I must inquire how it happened. I have not seen my men since I heard of the disaster. I suppose they will present plenty of plausible excuses, and will fasten the fault of the occurrence on anything but their own stupidity. Ah, captain, what do you think of my yacht?"

"Very fine lines, sir," replied the captain, as he and the mate gazed at the white steamer lying on the other bank of the main stream.

"If you will excuse me," said Stranleigh, "I will precede you on board, to inform cook and steward that three more plates are to be provided."

He and the doctor sprang up the steps; the motor boat gave itself a flick astern, and then the steam launch came to the floor of the gangway. Stranleigh welcomed his guests at the head of the stair, conducted captain and manager to easy-chairs aft, and ordered the deck steward to bring them sherry and bitters. He made a mental note of the fact that the mate had remained in the launch, and from this surmised that he had not succeeded in allaying the suspicions of captain and manager. He resolved to give them an opportunity of consulting alone together, wondering what their action would be when they had come to a decision regarding recent events.

"I must go below to see about the wine. Like a prudent owner I hold the keys of the wine bin myself. With a mixed crew you know the wisdom of such a course, captain."

"Yes, sir, I do," and with this the genial host went down the companion way with the doctor.

"What do you think of him?" muttered the captain, when they were thus left in solitude on the after deck.

"Oh, he's all right," said Frowningshield confidently. "I've met plenty of that kind before. A rich ass, good-natured, without too much brains, blowing in the money he has inherited."

"I'm not so sure of that," replied the captain.

"Oh, you're suspicious of everybody. He has blundered in here, and I dare say has amused himself as he said, shooting and chopping, and what not."

"Do you see," murmured the captain, "that this boat is fitted up for wireless telegraphy? That's the meaning of the line between the masts."

Frowningshield looked aloft.

"Oh, that's it, is it? Well, I don't see anything to worry about, even if it is so. I suppose plenty of yachts are fitted with Marconi apparatus nowadays. It certainly can't be much use to him here in West Africa."

"He might be in communication with some one outside."

"Out in the ocean, you mean? What would be the good of that?"

"I don't know," replied the captain. "This chap is too smooth-tongued to suit my book."

"What do you propose to do? Sink his craft and drown the lot of them?"

"No."

"What then?"

"Keep an eye on him, and not drink too much of his wine."

"You don't need to give that warning to me, captain. It would come more pat applied nearer home."

"You are right," admitted the captain. "If you notice me becoming talkative, just give me a nudge, will you? We must sit together at table."

"I think you are unduly suspicious, captain. This boat must have left England before we did."

"I'm not so sure of that. Some of these oceangoing yachts are very fast. She may be turbine-engined."

"Can't a sea-wise man like you tell whether she is or not by the look of her?"

"No, not from the outside. A question to one of the men would settle it."

"Ah, here comes a waiter with the drinks. Well, my man, this is a very nice yacht you have here."

"Yes, sir."

"Turbine engines, I suppose?"

"I don't know, sir. The engineer would be able to tell you."

"Yes, I suppose he would. How long is it since you left England?"

"Very sorry, sir, but I don't remember the date. The captain or the owner would know."

"Why, of course. Have you been stopping at many places since you quit the old sod?"

"Running in here and there, sir."

"Lisbon, or Teneriffe, perhaps?"

"Well, sir, I never had no head for them foreign places. They all look alike to me, sir. Plymouth, or Southampton, or Liverpool, sir, there's some difference between them."

"So there is, so there is," murmured Frowningshield, as the man respectfully withdrew.

"You see," said the captain, "even the stewards are on their guard."

"Oh, that's the noncommittal nature of the English servant. I imagine Stranleigh is by way of being a swell. There's something of that 'You-be-damned' air about him, in spite of his politeness, and the servants of such people know when they're in a good place, and keep their mouths shut. Still, I can't imagine a la-de-da chap like this, with a fashionable yacht, and a gang of gamekeepers, sent out to interfere with us. What can he do?"

"The steel prow of that motor boat didn't look fashionable," growled the captain. "She could sink the *Rajah*, loaded down as she is, in about ten seconds, although she'd crumple herself up if she tried it, and as to what he can do, look at what he has already done. The tumbling of all that timber in the river may have been an accident, as he says, but I don't believe it. It fitted the case of the mines too cursedly pat to suit me. He couldn't have hit it off better, and at less cost to himself, if he had studied for a year."

"Yes, it does take a bit of explaining, doesn't it? Still, there's nothing to be done with his crew of landlubbers. He daren't attack us; there are too many of us."

"I think you'll change your opinion before the week is out, Mr. Frowningshield. See what he's already done. He's cleared the river, and the waterway from the ocean to the mine is open. I tell you what it is, Mr. Frowningshield; there's been a miscalculation, and that man Schwartzbrod isn't as clever as you thought he was."

"Why do you say that?"

"Because, according to your story, it should have taken them a week or two to fit out another steamer, and by that time you expected to get the river protected, and erect a few forts. Now what has happened? Instead of that they have chartered the quickest yacht they could find in England, and they have cut in here ahead of us. This fellow's smooth talk about founding a colony is all balderdash. They've been spying upon us ever since we came here. The other fellows in England have taken their time in fitting up a steamer, or perhaps two steamers, or perhaps three. This chap has cleared the channel for them, and any fine morning you may see three or four ships in the offing, carrying perhaps three or four hundred men. *Then* what are you going to do?"

"There wouldn't be anything to do, of course, if all that happened. Nevertheless, all you say is mere surmise, but if the worst came to the worst they couldn't touch us. We're doing nothing illegal. I tell you old Schwartzbrod assured me he would get from the new owners a legal document covering everything he ordered done."

"But suppose he didn't get that document?"

"'We're both blooming prisoners, that's what we are!'"

"Oh, trust him! Of course he's got it, but even if he hadn't, we are doing nothing illegal. Here you are with your fortune made if you run three trips to Lisbon and back. You are quite safe, whatever comes, for you are bound to obey the orders of those who chartered the vessel. But apart from all that, we are out of British jurisdiction here, and you will be out of British jurisdiction at Lisbon. You've done nothing, and can do nothing, so long as you obey orders, that will render you liable to British law."

"I don't like the job a bit, Mr. Frowningshield; I tell you that straight."

"Nonsense, man. If any one is in danger, it's me, and I'm not afraid. You're protected by your ship's papers. You are under orders, and you must obey them. If anything is wrong, it is other people who must stand the brunt. It isn't criminal to sail a ship from Southampton to the West African coast, and it isn't criminal to make voyages to Lisbon and back. You are all right, who-ever's hurt, so don't get into a panic, captain, merely because a rich fool and his yacht appears to have discovered the Paramakaboo River."

The captain, sorely troubled, but somewhat comforted by the confident tone of his comrade, was absentmindedly turning the picture pages of the *Sphere*, which he had taken from the wicker table at his elbow. Suddenly something caught his eye.

"By the Lord, Frowningshield, look at the date of the *Sphere!* 24th of May, it says, and we sailed on the 13th—a mighty unlucky day I call it. He bought this paper more than a week after we left! I tell you, Frowningshield, we're done for. We're blooming prisoners, that's what we are!"

"'We're both blooming prisoners, that's what we are!'"

CHAPTER VI—AN ATTACK ON THE HIGH SEAS

Mr. manager frowningshield took up the copy of the *Sphere* in his hand, and gazed with troubled brow at this conclusive evidence of the date.

"Yes," he said at last, "he was in England a week later than we were, and must have come direct to this spot, passing us somewhere on the way; during the night, probably."

The captain was now standing up, his fists clenched.

"What do you propose to do?" inquired the manager.

"I should like to know first whether we are here as his guests or his prisoners. We were fools to have accepted his invitation without giving ourselves time to think and consult."

"But, hang it all, captain, he came on us so unexpectedly that there was no time to plan, or even to suspect. He seemed to speak so honestly and straightforwardly, and was so ready with his explanation that even up to a moment ago I believed he was but a blameless tourist, with, eccentric tastes, and the money to indulge them; a craze for big game shooting, like so many of them toffs have, and, of course, that kind of a man is mouching all over the world. You meet them everywhere: South America, Africa, Asia. Of course he's got us aboard here, and could steam away past your ship, and my settlement, with us two flung down the hold, and helpless, just as I put away that Scotch engineer on the *Rajah* at Southampton. By Jove, I shouldn't wonder a bit but that's what's in his mind: taking a leaf out of my own book. We would have no chance of self-defense with so many men on board, and our steam launch could not keep within sight of him if this boat has turbine engines. The mines are exploded, and the way is clear."

"Don't you think your men would give her a shot as she went by?"

"Not unless I was there to command them. I've left nobody in authority. I wonder what he's doing so long down below? If we are his guests, he should be here to entertain us."

"He is probably giving his orders," said the captain gloomily. "We are trapped, my boy. He wouldn't leave us this long to consult together unless he was sure of us."

"Why hasn't your mate come up from the launch?"

"I told him to stay there until I called him. You see, I had my doubts of this man from the first. If he attempts to lay hands on us, I'll shout to the mate to cut for it."

"What good could that do?" protested the manager. "The motor boat can overtake our launch even if she were half way to camp."

"Ah, here he comes," said the captain, as Stran-leigh, debonair and smiling, appeared at the head of the companion way. "I'll settle the question whether we are prisoners or not within two seconds."

"I hope you'll excuse me," began Stranleigh, coming forward, "but you are the first guests I have had the pleasure of receiving aboard since I left England, and I wish my to do his best, so I took the liberty of giving special orders for our lunch, and the gong will ring, they tell me, in about a quarter of an hour."

"I am very sorry, Mr. Stranleigh," replied the captain, "but I am a little anxious about my ship, so I have told my mate to remain in our launch, and I must ask you to excuse me. I cannot remain to lunch."

"Dear me, I'm sorry," said Stranleigh. "Why is that? What harm can come to your steamer?"

"Well, I've seen those logs piled up still very close to the brink of the river, and I fear if they tumbled down also, coming end on upon us, they might do the *Rajah* some damage."

"My men tell me," Stranleigh reassured him, "that there's no further danger of more logs getting into the river. Still, they are such fools that they may possibly be mistaken, and I quite share and sympathize with your anxiety. By the way, did any of the other logs damage your boat?"

"That I don't know yet. Some of them certainly struck her."

"Then, captain, you must let me pay for whatever damage has been done; yes, and overpay, because, after all, I am the man responsible.

Of course, you see, when we came up the river, there was no ship there, and no sign of any settlement. Still, that does not excuse my not having kept a better outlook. If the timber struck the steamer, is it likely the damage will be serious?"

"That, of course, I cannot tell without examination," replied the master of the *Rajah*.

"Well, captain, we come of a sporting race. I'll give you a hundred pounds here in gold, win or lose. If the damage is a thousand pounds, then you've lost. If there's no damage at all, you've won a hundred pounds. Come, captain, what do you say?"

"If no damage has been done, Mr. Stranleigh, I don't want any money from you. Even if the steamer is hurt, I am not sure I should have a valid claim against you. After all, the affair was an accident."

"Are you satisfied to give me a quit claim for a hundred pounds, cash down?"

"I'll be quite satisfied if you excuse me from attending luncheon, and allow me to go back to my ship."

"Oh, certainly, but I'd like you to take the money. Can't you send the mate, and order him to come back and report to you? It's a pity to miss a meal, you know."

"I'd feel safer if I went myself."

"Yes, I know exactly how anxious you must feel, and in your place I should do the same. Very well, captain, the only point between us is the hundred pounds or not. To tell the truth, I shall not object to pay full compensation to your owners for what I have done. I imagine, however, so stanch a ship as yours has come to no harm. She lies bow upstream, and the current is not so strong down there as it is up here. The timber, I think, if it struck at all, would glance off, carrying away nothing but a bit of paint; but if you must go, I shall insist on your taking the hundred pounds."

"Take the money, captain," said the manager, looking up at him with a smile. It was evident that his fears had once more been overcome, but the captain was not so easily cajoled.

"Very well," he said, anxious to end the situation and learn whether he was to be let go or not.

"And now, Mr. Frowningshield," continued Stranleigh, turning to the manager, "let us settle all our financial affairs before lunch, so that we may enjoy our meal without the thought of commercialism at the hoard. You have seen the damage I have caused in your forest, thinking all the while it was my own property. Of course, if you were acting for yourself alone, I am certain I could drive a very easy bargain with you, but you are responsible for the care of these lands to the European syndicate you spoke of, and so, on its behalf, you must be just, rather than generous. At how much coin of the realm do you place my depredations? I know it would cost me a pretty penny if I committed so unforgivable a trespass in England."

"How many trees did you cut down, Mr. Stranleigh?"

"Oh, Lord knows! Twenty, thirty, forty, fifty, sixty, or a hundred perhaps. That can easily be discovered. We'll send a man across in the motor boat to count the stumps."

"Oh, it isn't worth while. Would you be content to part with another hundred pounds?"

"Done; and you've let me off cheaply, Mr. Frowningshield. Just pardon me a moment until I get the money," and once more he disappeared down below.

But all this had not changed in the least the captain's apprehension.

"He's gone to give the signal," he said.

"Well, you know, captain, I've a great regard for you, yet I cannot find it possible to distrust the faith of that young man. He may be a fool, but he's a gentleman. I don't believe he would invite three men to a feast, and then imprison them. Now, I'm no fool, but then I'm no gentleman, either, and I'd do it in a minute, if I had an enemy in my power, yet I'm sure he won't. You'll see him come up with the money, and you'll miss a mighty good feed by going off to the *Rajah*."

"I'm willing to miss the meal, if I once get aboard my ship. I'll turn her round, and make for the ocean within the hour. You stop here as long as you can; all afternoon, if possible, and give the *Rajah* a chance to get out of sight before this fellow follows."

"But he can easily overtake you. Still, what could he do if he did? You surely don't expect him to seize your vessel?"

"I don't know what I expect, but I am afraid of him. I think him quite capable of following me to sea, and capturing the *Rajah*."

"Nonsense, that would be rank piracy. That would be a hanging matter. It would do him no good to sink you, and what could he do with the *Rajah* once he had her? There are too many witnesses on board. He wouldn't dare to sail into any port in the world. But then there's not the slightest danger of that. He's no pirate. The days of piracy are past. He may be a fool, but he's not such a fool as to try a trick like that."

"Will you stop here and give me a chance to get away?"

"Willingly."

"Very well, if I once get out of sight there are ten chances to one he can't catch me before I'm in the Tagus."

Stranleigh reappeared with some rolls of gold done up in paper, and these he divided equally between the captain and Frowningshield. The latter could not resist the temptation of asking a question.

"I've been looking at this illustrated newspaper, and I notice its date is very recent. You must have made a quick voyage from England, Mr. Stranleigh."

For a moment they had the young man on the hip, but he did not allow the knowledge of this to change the expression of his placid face. He took the journal in his hand, and looked at the date.

"Yes, they do these things quickly nowadays, but perhaps not so quickly as one unaccustomed to journalism would imagine. I believe that the illustrated weeklies are dated some time ahead, and I have been told they send forth their foreign editions as far in advance as possible. This, now, could have come from London, through by way of Paris to Lisbon, and reach that city probably several days before the date mentioned on the cover. I must ask the doctor where he bought this copy, whether at Lisbon or Teneriffe."

He flung the *Sphere* carelessly down on the table as if the matter, after all, was of no moment, and even Frowningshield, who was watching him like a detective of fiction, could distinguish no note of hesitation in his voice, nor catch any glance of annoyance from his eyes.

"Well, Mr. Stranleigh," said the captain, who was not equally successful in keeping an inflection of anxiety from his words, "I am very much obliged to you for your invitation, even though I cannot take advantage of it, so I shall bid you good-by."

"Oh, you're not away yet, captain," said Stranleigh, with a slight laugh, and the captain drew himself up with a little start of surprise. Stran-leigh walked to the head of the companion way, and said:

"Will you be as quick as you can down there?"

As his back turned on them, the captain grasped Frowningshield's wrist.

"He's playing with me like a cat with a mouse," he whispered.

"Nonsense," replied the other. "Your nerves have gone wrong. He's as transparent as glass."

Stranleigh turned, followed this time by a steward carrying a hamper,

"I don't like to think of your losing your lunch, captain," he said, "so I've had them put up a basketful for you and the mate on your way to the *Rajah*. There is in the hamper several bottles of champagne that I think will commend itself to you, or to any other judge of a good vintage, and there is also a box of cigars. If these weeds do not elicit the highest commendation I'll insist that you bestow on me a better box the next time we meet. So good-by, captain, and good luck to you. May you sail the high seas prosperously and safely. Here's hoping I shall meet you again when you are not in such a hurry."

Basket and hamper had been placed in the launch, and Stranleigh waved his hand at the captain and mate as their craft steamed out into the current and made for the mining camp.

The gong sounded out at last.

"Well, Mr. Frowningshield," said the young man, returning from the side, "if you're as hungry as I am, you'll enjoy this meal. Come along."

The manager did enjoy the meal, and they lingered long over the consuming of it, coming up on deck after it was over to indulge in coffee, liquors, and cigars. The manager fell under the charm of the young man's conversation, and began to revise his first estimate that his host was a fool. He had drunk but sparingly of the generous wine, yet in the glow of contentment which it produced he laughed quietly to himself now and then at the unfounded fears of the captain, which had cause him to run away from so excellent a repast.

"If this is a cigar from a similar box to the one you gave the captain, the old man is to be congratulated."

"Yes, it is. The captain, of course, will see civilization long before you do, and so can provide himself with any variety of the weed he fancies; but you, in this out-of-the-world place, are not so fortunate, therefore I must beg of you to accept six boxes in remembrance of the enjoyable time I have spent in your society."

"Why, Mr. Stranleigh, I'm awfully much obliged, and I may tell you at once I am not going to refuse. A man doesn't get a present like that every year of his life, worse luck."

"Then to make up the average, Mr. Frowning-shield, you must let me add a few cases of our champagne."

"Really, you are most kind. I don't know how to thank you."

"Don't attempt it, I beg of you."

A steward approached and presented Stranleigh with a sealed envelope, which, begging the pardon of his guest, he tore open, saying:

"I give all my orders in writing, so that there can be no mistake, and I rarely receive verbal reports from any one."

"A good idea," said Frowningshield.

"Yes, it prevents disputes afterwards."

He read to himself the penciled words of the telegrapher who had transcribed a wireless message from the hilltop.

"The *Rajah* is turning round, and is evidently about to depart."

Stranleigh, with a pencil, wrote on the back of the letter the following dispatch to Mackeller.

"Report once more if the *Rajah* actually sails; then take with you anything you don't want to leave, and come down to the water. The motor boat will be waiting for you. Come aboard at the prow, and get immediately out of sight in the forecastle, for sitting aft with me is the man who kicked you down into the hold, and I don't wish him to recognize you."

Giving this to the waiting steward, Stranleigh resumed conversation with his guest, who showed no desire to depart. Shortly after came the second message: "The Rajah has sailed. Send motor boat now."

Stranleigh folded up the sheet of paper, and handed it to the steward.

"Give that to the captain," he said, and a few minutes later the purr of the motor boat was heard leaving the ship. The sound aroused Frowningshield.

"Are you sending away the motor boat?" he asked. "As our steam launch has not returned, I fear I must depend on you for getting me down to the camp."

"Oh, that's all right," replied Stranleigh easily. "The boat isn't going far; just to pick up two of my men who've been prospecting in the hills. In fact, this is the end of my trespass, for there is little use in my gazing on a Promised Land that has been promised to somebody else. As for the motor boat, and getting to camp, I can take you there more comfortably than on that little craft. You see, there's nothing further to keep me here, as I have said, unless I can make terms with your syndicate, and that very likely would not suit my book, because cheapness of land was one of my objects in coming so far. If your syndicate expects to find valuable minerals on this property, they are not likely to sell any of their holdings to me at such a price as I should care to pay, so I think I shall cast off and away, but whether I shall go north or south will depend on circumstances when I get out to sea."

"What, you are not going to sail to-night, are you?" said Frowningshield, sitting up.

"Yes, there's no use in stopping here any longer. Do you happen to know any place along the coast which would be suitable as a colonizing place for Englishmen? I should like it to resemble this as much as possible: hills, a large flow of pure water, free from any fever swamps, and good soil."

"No, Mr. Stranleigh, this is the only portion of Africa I am acquainted with."

"It's very likely the captain of the *Rajah* may be able to give me some hints. He has probably knocked around the world a bit, and doubtless has kept his eyes open. I wish I had thought of asking him before he left whether or not he knows this coast. Besides, I would like to learn for certain if I have damaged his ship. It's a good thing she wasn't facing the other way, otherwise a log might have wrecked rudder or screw, or both."

"I am afraid," stammered Frowningshield, "that you won't see the captain again. He was very anxious to be off, and I rather fancy by this time he's well out at sea."

"Ah, in that case," remarked Stranleigh indifferently, "I shall be consoled by the assurance that his steamer is uninjured."

In due time the motor boat returned, and its occupants entered the yacht without being seen by their master's guest. The motor boat was hoisted on board, and the captain, coming aft, said:

"Any further orders, sir?"

"Yes. Plymouth, if you please. And, captain, just stop on your way at the camp, which I am informed is on the left-hand bank of the river. Draw up at the landing if there is one; if not, perhaps Mr. Frowningshield's launch will be waiting for him. There are some packages to go ashore."

The steamer proceeded down the river with just enough speed on to give her steering way. Frowningshield sat very silent, but his host made up with loquacity for the other's taciturnity. He told entertaining stories, and related odd experiences, and all with a delicate courtesy, as if his guest was the most honored of men, instead of being merely an adventurer and a marauder on a gold quest.

The captain drew up expertly at the landing. Nothing was to be seen of the *Rajah* that so lately had been berthed there. In spite of the fact that they saw their boss stepping ashore, large groups of men had ceased work, and were standing twenty or thirty yards back from the landing, viewing with eyes of wonderment the trim white steamer that had come out of the wilderness. Frowning-shield stepped ashore like a man in a dream, and a couple of stewards placed the cases of champagne and the boxes of cigars on the rock beside him. Lord Stranleigh leaned against the rail, and bade farewell to the manager.

"Wouldn't you like to come on to Plymouth with us?" he said. "Penny all the way. County Council express boat. No stop between Chelsea and London Bridge."

"God knows I wish I could," said Frowning-shield, with a deep sigh.

"Well, at least," cried Stranleigh cheerfully, "we've had one pleasant afternoon, and I'm more than grateful for your company. I hope that you will find valuable minerals on this spot; a second Klondike or Kimberley in either gold or diamonds. Somehow I think you'll be successful, and so I'll leave you my best wishes. Good-by, good-by."

The steamer was moving off down the river as Stranleigh waved his hand at the choice gang of ruffians that manned the highest outcrop of the reef.

"After all," he murmured to himself, "they're Englishmen, poor devils, and we're all a long way from home!"

The manager standing there on the rock suddenly bethought himself, and raised his hat. A cheer broke forth from the outlaws, and they waved aloft tattered caps.

"Pull the whistle, captain, with a hip-hip-hip-hurrah," and the siren sounded across the delta.

The manager stood for a long while watching the retreating boat, with his hands clasped behind him.

"By God," he said, "I don't know what to make of that man! I believe the captain's right, and that he'll capture the *Rajah* before nightfall, yet he'll have no shot from my cannon."

The Woman in White, as soon as she was out of sight of the camp, made record time to the coast, traversed the deep channel between the river and the sea with some caution, then struck straight out to the west. The sun was still about two hours above the western ocean. Far to the north the *Rajah* could be seen keeping closer inshore than seemed quite safe, the captain's idea being doubtless to get out of sight behind the first headland he might encounter. The heavily laden boat was burning up coal with reckless prodigality, the slight wind from the shore carrying out to sea a great black banner of smoke. Stranleigh walked forward to the captain.

"Can you overtake him before sunset?" he asked.

"I think so, sir."

"Well, I imagine our best plan is to convince him as speedily as possible that he can't run away from us. I don't like to see him wasting coal like that. Coal is more valuable than the ore he carries until we reach Teneriffe. Full speed ahead, captain."

The hum of the turbines rose and rose, and the trembling of the yacht perceptibly increased as the sharp prow clove through the waters with the speed of a torpedo-boat destroyer. The steward, setting out cups and saucers for tea, on a wicker table, found some difficulty in keeping the jingling dishes from catastrophe. The *Rajah* had about four hours the start, and had probably worried away thirty knots of the long route she was to travel. Higher and higher she seemed to rise in the water, and the sun was still a good quarter of an hour above the horizon when *The Woman in White* came tearing up alongside to landward of her, carried now by her own momentum, for the turbines had been stopped some distance away. Apparently everybody on board was leaning over the rail watching the amazing speed of the swanlike craft, white and graceful, as she gradually slowed down. Stranleigh recognized the anxious face of the captain, and shouted up at him:

"Tell your stokers to economize on that coal." The captain replied truculently:

"No one gives orders on this steamer but me."

"Quite right," replied Stranleigh, with less imperiousness than had barbed his first shout. "That's why I'm asking you to give the command."

The captain, after a moment's hesitation, sent the order below, then turned again to the white vessel, which was now keeping exact time with his own black one.

"Captain," said Stranleigh, in his ordinary tone of voice, "both Frowningshield and myself were very sorry you could not lunch with us, so perhaps you will be good enough to come aboard this yacht and dine with me."

"A captain cannot leave his ship," curtly replied the master of the *Rajah*.

"Ordinarily, no, but this is an exceptional case. I've got a letter for you, captain."

"Then why didn't you give it to me at noon?"

"Oh, come now, a man can't think of everything when he is overjoyed at receiving an expected and very welcome guest. You must admit, captain, that once I undertook the work of ocean postman, I lost no time in giving you the double knock. I don't think there's anything in these waters would have overhauled you so quickly as I have done. Won't you then make an exception, and honor us with your presence?"

"No, I will not. If, as you say, you've got a letter for me, I'll throw down a line for it."

"Well, on the face of it, that seems fair. A man in England drops you a line, and you drop a line for his line. Nevertheless, this letter, although addressed to you, I do not intend to part with. There are several documents in my pocket which I'd like to show you, and I wish to make some explanations that will interest you."

"Look here, Mr. Stranleigh, I'm captain aboard this steamer, and I'm on the high seas. I warn you, before witnesses here, that any interference on your part is piracy. I shall not come aboard your steamer, nor shall I allow any one from your steamer to come aboard of me. I take orders from none but my own masters, the owners of this ship. I am now under their orders, and acting upon them. I won't stand any interference."

"Again I say quite right, captain. Your sentiments are admirable, and your views of nautical duty are correct. Nevertheless, it is necessary that you and I should enjoy a quiet talk together, and I ask you to favor me by coming aboard."

"Well, I won't."

"Then, as the mountain wouldn't come to Mahomet, Mahomet went to the mountain. I ask your permission to go aboard your vessel."

"I shan't give it. I've told you that before. Now, sheer off, or I'll put a cannon ball into your engine room."

"Oh, have you got a cannon ball on board? How jolly! We are entirely unarmed so far as ordnance is concerned, but I'd like to say, captain, that the chances are ten to one your cannon ball wouldn't do much harm. You might even plant a floating mine in front of *The Woman in White*, and although it probably would blow her prow up, yet I think, crablike, I could crawl backward to the nearest port, as the White Star liner *Suevic* made her way from the Lizard to Southampton."

"Are you going to sheer off, sir."

"No, and you are not going to fire, either, captain. It isn't etiquette at sea to shoot cannon balls at a man until you have finished the cigars he has presented to you. I dislike very much to allude to my own gifts in this way, but still I wish you to understand that I am well versed in nautical law."

"I want to get along with my voyage, Mr. Stranleigh, unmolested."

"Why, bless your tarry heart, captain, get along with your voyage. If you can run away from us, don't let me put any obstacle in your path."

"Will you sheer off, sir."

"Certainly not. I'm quite within my rights. This part of the ocean belongs as much to me as to the *Rajah*. I'm not delaying you in the least, and all your talk of interference is mere humbug. If I ran my craft close enough to endanger yours, you might have a right to object; but I call your attention to the fact that we are under perfect control, and I can keep the distance between the ships to an inch. If I went farther away, I should be unable to converse with you without straining my throat, which I decline to do. Now, you will neither come aboard my vessel, nor allow me to go aboard yours."

"That's right."

"Well, I don't think it is. Nevertheless, you force me to do what I should much rather, for your sake, not do, and that is I am compelled to read your letter, and the documents I have referred to, in the hearing of your crew and my own."

"You may read what you like to the crew."

"Captain, I ask you to reconsider that dictum. I grant that you might honestly have made such a remark on any other voyage you have ever taken during your long seafaring life, except this one. Just think for a moment. Don't reply rashly, and be assured that I mean no harm to you, nor to anybody else aboard your ship. Quite the contrary. What I intend to do will be greatly to your advantage, and to that of every man who is with you."

When Lord Stranleigh made reference to his present voyage, the captain, who had been leaning against the rail, stood up suddenly. The men were whispering with one another. The captain saw that Stranleigh had taken from his pocket several envelopes, and stood there awaiting his reply. At last the captain said huskily:

"Will you come aboard alone, sir?"

"Oh, quite alone, of course, since it is your wish, or you can come aboard here with half a dozen or a dozen men as your bodyguard, if you like. Bring the cannon, too, if it makes you feel any safer."

"I'd rather you came aboard here, sir."

"Very good. Fling over a slightly stronger line than you'd have sent down for the letter, and I'll be with you in a jiffy."

"But how am I to know some others won't climb up?"

"Well, hang it, arm your men with handspikes, and knock 'em down again. Don't keep me waiting here all night. It will be dark very soon, and I shan't occupy more than ten minutes of your time. You seem spoiling for a fight, but I can't accommodate you. I'm a man of peace, and that's why I shudder when you speak to me of cannon. I swear I'll tell Sir Henry Campbell-Bannerman and President Roosevelt the way you're behaving. You're a positive danger on the high seas, with your ultimatums, and your shots through the engine room, and all that. Heave over a line, and get your men to watch that the yacht doesn't spring aboard of you. No wonder we English are disliked for our browbeating."

The captain seemed rather ashamed of his fears in face of this bantering, and besides, some of his crew had laughed, which still further disconcerted him. A rope fell coiling through the air, and came slap on deck.

"Hang tight aloft there," cried Stranleigh, as he jerked the rope taut, swung himself free of his own boat, and clambered up the black cliff of the *Rajah* hand over hand, feet against the side like a monkey.

CHAPTER VII—THE CAPTAIN OF THE "RAJAH" STRIKES OIL

THE captain strode gloomily to the evil-smelling den he called the cabin, and Stranleigh went down the steps with him, seating himself at the table.

"Now, captain," he began, "can we be overheard?"

"No, sir."

"Well, I come here as your friend. I want to save you, if possible."

"Save me?"

"Yes."

"I don't need any saving."

"Yes, you do, and a good deal of it. I thought at first that Frowningshield was the sole culprit, and that you were merely an innocent victim. I learned to-day that such was not the case; in fact, I surmised it before, because when you assisted in planting those mines across the Paramakaboo River you must have known you were committing a capital offense."

"Then it wasn't an accident; you *did* send down the logs?"

"Of course I did."

"You watched us ever since we arrived there?"

"Yes, I came from England for that purpose. I left a week after you did, and was there a week before you, more or less. My man, Mackeller, whom you kidnapped on board this steamer at Southampton——"

"I didn't kidnap him, sir. It was Frowning-shield."

"Oh, I know all about it. Mackeller is on my boat now, within three hundred yards of where you are sitting. He was up on the hilltop with a telescope, scrutinizing every action of yours since you landed."

"But I'm compelled to obey orders."

"Oh, no, you aren't. If you are ordered to do a criminal action, you must not only refuse, but you are in honor bound to give information to the authorities."

"I had nothing to do with putting Mackeller into the hold. Frowningshield put him in, and I didn't know he was there till we were more than a day out. It was me insisted he should be sent ashore with the pilot. Frowningshield wanted to take him with us."

"That's neither here nor there, captain. Of course, whenever you knew a man had been kidnapped in that way aboard your ship, you should have turned, made straight back to Southampton, giving information to the authorities. But even if such an unlawful action did not arouse your suspicions you must have known perfectly well when you planted those mines that it wasn't toy balloons you were putting in the water. It's too late to pretend innocence. You've been bribed to commit a crime."

"The floating mines weren't set in English waters."

"My dear sir, your offense is against international law. No man is allowed to place floating mines in a river up which a British steamer may ascend, and so far as that is concerned, you deliberately put them there to wreck a British steamer. You are at this moment commanding a pirate ship filled with stolen ore."

"I know nothing about that, sir. This ship was chartered, and I was told by my owners to obey the orders of them that chartered her, and that's old Schwartzbrod and his gang."

"We're merely losing time, captain. You talk about charters and owners. Well, I am the owner of the *Rajah*. I bought her from Sparling & Bilge."

"So *you* say. That's nothing to do with me. Even if you bought the ship, you are bound by law to carry out the charter. Till a charter runs out and isn't renewed, owners are helpless. I obey the charter while it holds, and as long as I do that I'm doing nothing wrong."

"You are perfectly well aware of what you are doing. I am convinced of that. You were not born yesterday. Now, you are not sailing toward Portugal, you are sailing toward a policeman, and it is from that policeman I wish to save you."

"Oh, yes, you'd like to get possession of the ship and cargo for yourself, wouldn't you?" sneered the captain.

"Yes, exactly."

"Well, you won't get it!" cried the master angrily, bringing his huge fist down on the table. "Talk to me of thieving! What are you? Why, you're a pirate, that's what you are. I said so to Frowningshield, and he wouldn't believe me. He thought you wouldn't dare come aboard of me on the high seas; that you knew better. You and your policeman! Why, damn it all, I'd be justified in hanging you from the yardarm!"

"You couldn't do that, captain," protested Stranleigh, with great mildness.

"Why couldn't I?"

"Because those two masts of yours are not provided with yardarms. You might possibly hang me from the funnel, or allow me to dangle in chains from one of the arms of your steam crane, but that's all."

"Why don't you and your gang of ruffians climb aboard here like real pirates, and make me walk the plank?"

"I have climbed aboard like a real pirate, and I am going to make you walk the plank."

"The devil you are!" cried the captain, rising, his two clenched hands resting on the table, his naturally florid face still further flushed with wrath. "I'll show you—I'll show you what we do to men of your kind that dare to come aboard a ship on the high seas."

"Sit down, my dear man, sit down," pleaded Stranleigh soothingly. "Don't bluster. What's the use of making a fuss? Let's discuss the thing amicably."

"Make me walk the plank, will you?" roared the captain, a-quiver with resentment.

"Oh, well, well, if you object, of course that puts a different complexion on the matter. I thought that walking the plank was a customary nautical amusement. I seem to have been misled by friend

Clark Russell. If it isn't etiquette, let's say no more about it. Do sit down, captain."

But the captain wouldn't sit down. His eyes glared, his face grew redder, and his lips quivered with animosity.

"You come alongside with your toy yacht!"

"It's a toy, captain, that spins along a little faster than this old tub."

"You and your jackanapes dressed up like naval officers, dare to come aboard o' me."

"That's splendid, captain. I like that phrase, 'aboard o' me.' I'm delighted to have Clark Russell corroborated from your mouth. Yes, I come aboard o' you. What then?"

"What then? Why, then you try to browbeat me in my own cabin, on my own ship. Who the devil do you think you are, I'd like to know?"

"I am Earl Stranleigh of Wychwood."

The captain now, without being told, slowly relapsed into his chair, and gazed across the table at the young man. That latent respect for the aristocracy which permeates even the most democratic of his Britannic Majesty's subjects caused an instant collapse of the truculence which had threatened an abrupt conclusion to the conference. Curiously enough, the honest captain never thought of questioning the statement, which had been made in a quiet, but very convincing tone.

"Earl Stranleigh!" he gasped.

"Yes; of Wychwood. We always insist on the Wychwood, though I'm sure I don't know why, for there isn't another Lord Stranleigh, and Wychwood is far from being the most important of my estates. Still, there you have it, captain. English life is full of incongruities."

"The *rich* Lord Stranleigh?" questioned the captain, with an accent on the adjective.

"I've just told you there's only one."

"Then why in the name of Neptune are you pirating on the high seas? Is *that* the way you made your money?"

"No, my money was more or less honestly accumulated by my ancestors, but I think their method was highway robbery rather than piracy. The looting of land that didn't belong to them seemed to occupy their spare time, and so, what with the rise of manufacturing cities in the midlands, on portions of our property, the discovery of coal mines, and what not, my family prospered better than it deserved, and here am I the twentieth-century representative of it."

"If that is so, why the deuce are you meddling in this affair?"

"Because I like to see a man minding his own business. The ship which you so worthily sail is mine. I bought her a few days after you left Southampton. Here is the deed of transfer, and here is the letter I spoke of, written to you by Messrs. Sparling & Bilge, informing you that I am the new owner, that I shall be responsible for your pay hereafter, and as a consequence they will be much obliged, as, indeed, so shall I, if you do what I tell you."

The captain read the documents with slow care, then looked up.

"It's Sparling & Bilge's signature all right, and nobody knows it better than I do, but what about the cargo? Do you intend to unship at Lisbon?"

"No, I intend to run it to Plymouth."

"But even if the ship's yours, the cargo isn't."

"Surely you knew they were stealing the ore, captain?"

"They told me they had a right to it for three months. Mr. Schwartzbrod showed me papers to that effect. That's why they were in such a hurry. Wanted to get as much out in the time as they could, and offered me a bonus of five thousand pounds over and above my wages if I ran three voyages to Lisbon, and two thousand for each extra voyage within the time."

"Then, captain, why didn't they concentrate their energies on the mining of the ore, and not bother with the mining of the river?"

"Why, Frowningshield told me that they were on the lookout for some pirates that was going to interfere with them. We didn't intend to blow up any vessels unless they were determined to come up the river in spite of us. That's why we didn't put the mines at the mouth of the river. On the high ground west of the camp, Frowning-shield had two men on watch all the time. If they saw any ship approach, they were to go down the river in a boat that was kept below the mines, and order the steamer to go back. If the captain wouldn't go back, then he came on at his own risk."

"I see. And did Frowningshield tell his men to inform captain and crew that the river was mined?"

"I don't know."

"Now, captain, talking as one seafaring man to another, didn't all this, in conjunction with the large sums of money promised you, strike you as rather fishy? Did this appear to you an honest trading?"

"Well, earl, I've sailed to all parts of distant seas, and I've known things done that would have looked mighty queer in Southampton Harbor, and yet they were all right as far as ever I knew. Things happen in the South Seas that would seem rather odd in Bristol Channel, you know."

"You didn't think you were running any risk, then?"

"Oh, risk! A seafaring man runs risks every time lie leaves port. If this was a risk, there was good money at the end of it, and that isn't always the case when a man ships on a tramp steamer nowadays, what with everything cut to pieces by foreign competition. You see, earl, men born to money don't always appreciate what people will do who're trying to pile up a little cash against their old age. I've got a wife and family in a hired house in Southampton—three girls I've got at home, earl, and girls is helpless left poor—not to mention my old woman."

The captain's eyes took on a dreamy, far-away look that seemed to penetrate and question the future. He had, for the moment, forgotten the young man sitting opposite him, and went on as if talking to himself.

"There's a piece of land running down to Southampton water—five acres and a bit more. Somebody built a cottage there and put up a flagpole on the lawn in front. Then they got tired of it, and it's for sale. A thousand pounds they want for the place, everything included. There's a few trees, and there's outhouses; splendid spot to raise chickens. Then there's a veranda in front, and an oldish man might sit in an easy-chair smoking his pipe, and see the American liners come sailing past. And my family's living in a rented house on a back street. I've always wanted that bit of land, earl, but never had the money to spare, and when I come to settle down, like as not somebody else will own it, and we couldn't afford it, anyhow. Risks? Of course there's risks, but when I think of that little cottage—well, I took the risk, earl."

"My dear captain," said the earl softly, "your bit of land makes me ashamed of myself, and of my moral lectures. I have so much land, and others have so little. Here's a hard-working man like you, landless, and here's a loafer like me with thousands of acres! Hang me if I wouldn't turn Radical were it not for the awful example of William Thomas Stead. Well, captain, that plot of land is yours from this moment. If somebody else has bought it in your absence, we'll evict them. I'll go bail that old Schwartzbrod will pay you all he promised whether you make the voyages or not. Indeed, you are not going to make the voyages, as a matter of fact. I don't believe Schwartzbrod ever intended to keep his promise, and I very much doubt if you could collect. Now, I'm an excellent collector, and I think I can persuade Schwartzbrod to plead for the privilege of paying you. You see these city men are much too sharp for simple, honest chaps like you and me. After you had done their work, they would have left you in the lurch if you were caught, or cheated you out of your compensation if you escaped. You may depend upon it, Schwartzbrod and his crowd have done everything in the most legal manner. Indeed, as a matter of fact, the last time I saw him he wheedled a document from me which I have reason to believe covers the villainy of this expedition. I do not in the least doubt that if I took the case into the law courts I'd get beaten. That's why I preferred to fight the case on the high seas, where an injunction can't be served till it's too late. You and I, captain, are not shrewd enough to be a match for these rascals."

There was almost a smirk of self-satisfaction on the captain's face as he found himself thus linked with a man of Lord Stranleigh's rank.

"Well, earl," he said, "what do you want me to do?"

They were interrupted by the heavy steps of the mate coming down the stairs.

"What do you want?" roared the captain. "Get out of here."

"Beg pardon, sir," explained the mate, "but they're getting uneasy on the yacht, and want to know what's become of the boss."

"Just excuse me for a moment, captain," said Stranleigh, "and I'll speak to them. You know you did rather tyrannize over us when we first hailed you, and they probably think you've Mac-kellered me. I rather flatter myself I've made a pun there, for 'keller' is the German for cellar." The young man sprang lightly up the steps, and went over to the bulwarks.

"Is it all right, sir?" shouted Mackeller.

"All right, thank you."

"It's getting dark, you know. Hadn't I better heave a revolver up to you, and if they try any tricks you can fire it off, and we'll be aboard before you can say 'Schwartzbrod.'"

"Ah, Mackeller, Mackeller, you're always thinking of deadly weapons and acts of piracy! No wonder I get a bad name in marine circles. Everything's going smoothly, and I expect to be with you within ten minutes."

Stranleigh returned to the cabin, where he found the captain sitting, staring into vacancy. Some one had lit an odorous oil lamp.

"Well, captain, before answering your question, I wish to say that I am interested in mercantile traffic aside from my ownership of the *Rajah*. Before I left England I reserved for you the berth of captain on a new steamer called the *Wychwood*, twice the size of this boat, that is intended for the South American trade. I think she will be ready for you by the time we reach Plymouth, and the moment we are in Plymouth I shall hand you a check for a thousand pounds to secure that bit of land by Southampton water. What sort of a crew have you aboard here? A mutinous lot, or easy going?"

"Oh, the crew's all right, earl. They're Devon men, most of them. It was a rough lot of passengers we took out under charge of

Frowning-shield, but they herded most by themselves, and held no truck with the crew. The crew's all right, sir."

"Do you think any of the crew knew what was going on?"

"No, I don't suppose anybody knew what was going on but me and Frowningshield."

"Would you like to have your present crew with you on the new steamer?"

"Yes, sir, I would."

"Officers, too?"

"Yes, I would. Officers, too."

"Very well, I want you to come aboard my yacht, and be captain of her from here to Plymouth. Take the mate with you, if you like, or any of the other officers, and take such of the crew as are not Devon men. I'll put some of my own fellows aboard in their place."

"You mean me to leave the ship, my lord?"

"Yes. The yacht's captain and mate will take the place of you and your mate."

The captain's face was a study of indecision and doubt.

"It doesn't seem quite right, my lord."

"Your late owners have told you to obey me, and I am your new owner. It is quite right. I have merely transferred you to the yacht as if I were transferring you to a ferry boat, in order to take you the more quickly to your new command. We'll reach Plymouth in a fortnight, or three weeks before the *Rajah* does. I'd rather you didn't go to Southampton, but if you think you can keep out of sight, I don't mind your running across there, seeing your family, and securing that property. Indeed, if the property is still in the market, and the house empty, there's no reason why you shouldn't move your people into it. You'll have time enough, then you can return to Plymouth, see to your new ship, and engage what men you need to supplement the *Rajah's* crew when she arrives."

The captain made no reply: bowed head and wrinkled brow showed that a mental conflict was going on.

"I suppose you are very well known in Southampton?"

"No," he said; "not so well known as you might think. I'm there for a little while, then off on a long voyage. Not as well known as might be."

"You see, captain, I'm determined to get out of old Schwartzbrod the money wherewith to pay not only you, but Frowningshield and his men. I don't intend to leave them marooned there while Schwartzbrod sits safe in London, so I wish no rumor of what has taken place to reach the ears of Schwartzbrod and his syndicate, therefore I don't want you to be seen and recognized by anybody, if possible, and if you are recognized I am anxious that you should not talk about what has occurred."

"I see. You want to get all the witnesses shipped off to South America. Well, you know, my lord, meaning no disrespect, your way of doing things seems a little fishy, too, as you said a while ago."

"Of course it looks fishy, but you must fight a whale with a shark if you haven't got a harpoon. I must either go to law, which is the harpoon, with old Schwartzbrod, who is the whale, or else adopt his own methods, and play the shark. You've got to choose which course of fish you're going to take, and you've got to give your order to the waiter now."

"Suppose I refuse, what will you do? Attempt to capture us?"

"Bless you, no. I'll merely follow you, just as a shark follows a doomed vessel. The moment you approach a port that contains a British consul, I'll dash on ahead, show my papers, and set the law in motion, which, as I have informed you, I am reluctant to do. The moment that happens I can't save you, captain. I don't know what the penalty is, or whether there is a penalty. Perhaps your obedience to orders may allow you to slip through the meshes of the net, and then again perhaps it won't. If it doesn't, then that little cottage on Southampton water, which was yours a moment ago, will never be occupied by your family. Oh, hang it all, I'm either coercing or bribing you now, whichever it is. You must make a free choice. Whatever happens, I'll buy that piece of land, and present it to your wife, if you will tell me where it is, and give me her address. Now, captain, make your choice: the whale or the shark."

The captain heaved a deep, almost a heartrending sigh, that seemed to come from the very bottom of his hoots. He rose slowly and ponderously, and stretched forth his hand.

"Lord Stranleigh," he said solemnly, as one about to cross the Rubicon, "Lord Stranleigh, I am ready to walk the plank."

When Lord Stranleigh emerged from the captain's cabin of the *Rajah,* and drew a long, satisfying breath of the sweet evening air outside, he saw that the moon had risen, while the glow from the sunset still tinted the western sky. The slight breeze from Africa had completely died away, and the sea lay around the two ships smooth as a polished mirror. At a word from Stranleigh the captain of the yacht drew her alongside the Rajah, and the engines of both steamers stopped. Captain Wilkie, forewarned, had all his belongings packed, and they were speedily swung aboard the black steamer. The captain of the Rajah, and his mate, flung their possessions into boxes, and thus the transfer was made without loss of time.

"Mackeller," said Stranleigh, "I fear that luxury is thrown away on you, and besides, experience on the yacht has shown you that there is little chance of anything exciting happening. It must discourage you to remember that none of your repeating rifles have even been unpacked, so I will cause the cases to be swung aboard the *Rajah,* with sufficient ammunition to massacre our entire naval force, and I'll give you six of my gamekeepers. You can either use the gamekeepers to shoot the crew, or arm the crew and eliminate the gamekeepers. I had intended to take the crew of the *Rajah* upon the yacht, and put the crew of the yacht on the *Rajah,* but I am so selfish that I cannot bring myself to trust those clumsy seafarers from a tramp steamer with the somewhat delicate organization of my yacht. Will you accept the commission, and sail for home on the comfortless *Rajah?"*

"I shall be delighted, sir," said Mackeller. "You see, I feel just a little uncertain about the wisdom of leaving Captain Wilkie unprotected with what is, after all, a strange crew. Their captain gives them a good character, but Captain Wilkie, who is a martinet in his way, may get at loggerheads with them, so it is well that he should have a bloodthirsty commander and irresistible force at his beck and call. But remember, Peter, that for every sailor you shoot, one of your gamekeepers must take to the sailoring trade, which might turn out inconvenient in a storm, so repress your war spirit until the captain orders it to belch forth. I imagine your frowning appearance as, resembling the German Emperor, you walk the deck, will quell any incipient mutiny in the bud, if buds are quelled. Nevertheless, it is safer to hold the rifles in the background in case of an emergency. So call for six volunteers from among my men, and then fling your trunk aboard the lugger, after which it will be good-by till I meet you again at Plymouth." When the exchange was completed the white yacht drew away from the tramp and speedily disappeared to the north like a ghost. Captain Wilkie watched her departure with regret, and was unhappy at his promotion to the unkempt and dirty tramp steamer, with her slouching crew, dressed like scarecrows. The new commander of the yacht felt equally out of place in this trim, scrupulously clean, nickel-plated, bride's-cake of a ship, while the sailors, in their spick-and-span natty uniforms, gave him the impression of being in a nightmare where an uncouth private had been placed in charge of a company of officers. As he was about the same size as Wilkie, the useful Ponderby, at Stranleigh's orders, fitted him out next morning in a gorgeous uniform which added to the beauty of his outward appearance without materially augmenting his inward comfort. However, the bluff captain understood his business, no matter what costume he wore, and Stranleigh, studying him very unobtrusively as the voyage went on, came to place a great confidence in him, and felt rather ashamed of the distrust that had caused him to transfer the captain from the *Rajah* to the yacht. Before a week was past, he was certain that this gruff sea dog would have taken the *Rajah* direct to Plymouth once he had given his word, quite as faithfully as Captain Wilkie was doing. Although Stranleigh said nothing of this trust, and even doubted if the simple old man had seen the reason of the change, he nevertheless resolved to make amends, though not in words. The weather throughout had been almost obtrusively gentle, and Stranleigh complained that the voyage was falsifying all of Clark Russell's novels. He grumbled to the doctor that his faith in Clark Russell was undergoing a tremendous strain.

"When we reach a dead calm in one of Clark Russell's novels," he said to the doctor, "we always know what to expect. Suddenly out of the west comes a ripping cyclone which lays us over on our beam ends. Then wild, blinding rain and utter darkness, lit up only by vivid flashes of lightning. Every one has to cling to whatever is nearest him: overboard go the chicken coops, and there is such a general pandemonium that the voice of command cannot be heard. Crash go the masts, funnels, and what not: we right ourselves, staggering under the mountainous waves, and find ourselves a dismantled hulk next morning, with the cook missing, and no hot rolls for breakfast. Now, in reality we have had evenings without a zephyr afloat, then follows a peaceful night, and morning comes with a maidenly blush, like that on a new-born rose. I imagine the ocean has improved since Clark Russell's time, or perhaps the Government weather bureau has regulated tilings. We are a wonderful people, doctor, and at last Britannia really does rule the waves."

Fast as his yacht was, the young man had become tired of the voyage. He yearned for his morning paper and a stroll down Piccadilly. When well across the placid Bay of Biscay, he called up one of his wireless telegraphers, and said to him:

"I say, my son, cannot you tune up your heavenly harp, and pull us some news down out of the sky? Aren't we within the Marconi range of civilization yet?"

"Yes, sir. Several private messages have come through, and some scraps of news, but nothing important. The chancellor of the exchequer is speaking in the House of Commons on some bill, so far as I understand it, to regulate the Bank of England."

"I fear that wouldn't be very exciting reading, my boy, and besides, I don't understand finance, and never did. Still, I'd welcome even the words of a politician this evening, so if the chancellor is still talking, write out what he says. And, by the way, if you get a chance to talk back, you might ask the horizon what races were on to-day, and which horses won. After all, it is encouraging to know that the chancellor of the exchequer is on his feet. That shows that old England is still a going concern. It seems a year since I was there."

The operator departed for the telegraphic cabin, and Stranleigh went on with his cigar and after-dinner coffee. Presently the young man returned with a grin on his face.

"He's at it again, sir," he said, and handed Stranleigh a sheet of paper headed:

"CHANCELLOR EXCHEQUER.

"During the past decade our bank rate has been in a state of constant fluctuation, changing many times, and ranging from two-and-a-half to seven per cent., a variation which has exercised anything but a beneficial effect upon business. The gold in the issue department of the Bank of England usually amounts to about thirty millions of pounds, which are shown to be inadequate to the needs of our time. On the other hand, the Bank of France rarely allows its reserve to fall below a hundred millions of pounds, with a consequence that the French bank rate remains steady at from two-and-a-half to three per cent., and has not risen to four per cent for thirty years. In the twelve months preceding the report of 1904 the bank rate of France had not been changed once, while our own bank rate had jumped from — —"

Here Stranleigh crumpled the paper into a ball in his hand, and flung it into the ocean.

"Great heavens!" he cried. "I wonder what kind of a brain revels in that sort of rot! And not a word about the races! What do these telegraphers imagine news is, anyhow?"

The ignorant young man little dreamed that the message he was reading would exercise an astounding influence on his own career on that day when the Bank of England was compelled by the new Act of Parliament to raise its reserve of gold from thirty millions of pounds to one hundred millions. A world-wide financial disturbance lay ahead which Stranleigh did not suspect any more than did the wise lawmakers who passed the bill by a large majority. Most of them, including his lordship, thought the races more important and interesting.

The captain strolled aft. More and more as the days went on the frivolous young man's liking for this veteran of the sea had increased, in spite of the fact that the captain had endeavored to carry away his gold mine.

"Sit down, captain," he cried. "What will you drink?"

"A cup of coffee, to keep me awake. I expect to be up all night, or at least till we pass the Ushant."

"Right you are, and coffee it is. Oh, by the way, I have changed my mind, and you must change your course. Instead of striking straight across from Ushant to Plymouth, steer your course up the Channel for Southampton."

"Very good, earl."

"And I've also changed my mind regarding that bit of land of yours."

"Oh, have you, earl?" said the captain, with a catch in his voice, and disappointment visible on his countenance.

"Yes, that's the reason we're going to Southampton. You will lay this yacht up—I think that is the nautical term—alongside your bit of land. As you know, I am anxious that you shouldn't be seen, and also that nobody aboard should have a chance to talk."

"I'll see to that, earl."

"My dear man, don't call me earl. I told you I was an earl in strict confidence. Haven't you noticed that everyone addresses me as 'sir,' and I don't even insist on that. We are all free and equal at sea, except the captain, who rules over us. When we reach Southampton water I'll go ashore in the motor boat, will call on the land agent, secure the estate of five acres, give the deeds to your wife, and invite her and the family to come up and view the cottage."

"She knows where it is, sir. We've often been there together."

"Then you'll grant no shore leave, not even to yourself. You'll keep the lads busy while I'm ashore. Take the yacht to the nearest coaling station, wherever it is, and fill her up with black diamonds. We may want to go to New York, for all I know. What time do you expect to pass Ushant?"

"About one bell, sir; half an hour after midnight."

"How long is the run from Ushant to Southampton?"

"We should do it easy in eleven hours."

"Then we'll reach there at noon to-morrow? Very good. You had better, perhaps, run me right up to Southampton, attend to the port formalities, see to the coaling, and be lying off your bit of property by six o'clock next evening. I'll stop the night at a hotel, so you needn't trouble about me. How large is your family, captain?"

"The three eldest are at sea, and the three girls at home with the missus."

"Three girls? Oh, that's jolly! Very well, I think we've everything arranged. You will see that the motor boat is ready for me at the landing both to-morrow afternoon and all next day. I shall probably want to run up the bay to the bit of land, or down, whichever it is. I suppose you can point it out to me as we pass?"

"Oh, yes, sir. I never enter or leave Southampton without looking at that bit of ground."

"Very well. At about five o'clock p.m. day after to-morrow I shall invite the missus and the three girls to take a trip with me in the motor boat. Arriving there I shall hand the keys and the deeds to the lady of the house, and if you come ashore I'll introduce you to the family. You may stop all night ashore. Next morning take the yacht, and navigate her slowly round to Plymouth. There you may give everybody shore leave, but don't overdo it. You understand what I want, which is that no man shall talk about the mine in West Africa or the transfer in midocean, so I expect you to keep your section of the crew in hand. I can answer for my fellows. Oh, yes, by the way, I'll take my woodmen off at noon to-morrow, together with all that are left of my gamekeepers, and send them home, including the excellent Ponderby, so you will have none to deal with except those belonging to the yacht."

The Woman in White did even better than the captain anticipated, and landed her owner in Southampton at ten minutes to eleven. He bade farewell to his men, and dispatched them to their homes, none the poorer for their long voyage. He visited the land agent's office, transacted his business within ten minutes, drew his check, and told the manager to have the papers ready by twelve o'clock next day. Then he went to the back street, and knocked at the number the captain had given him. The door was opened by a buxom young woman, in whose flashing eyes he recognized her father.

"Well, my dear," he said, chucking her under the chin, "are you the gallant captain's daughter, as we say in the revised version of 'Pinafore'?"

The girl drew back in righteous anger, and if a dagger glance of the eyes could have slain, he would have been in danger, but the callous young man merely laughed.

"Mother at home?" he asked.

"Who are you?" demanded the offended girl.

"That's the same question your father asked me. It's a secret, and I'll tell it only to your mother."

At this moment the mother, hearing the high tones of her daughter, and fancying something was wrong, appeared in the hall; a stout, elderly woman, who frowned at the tall, nattily dressed stranger.

"My name is Stranleigh, madam, and I am by way of being a shipowner. Your husband is one of my captains."

"He is nothing of the sort. He is captain of the *Rajah*.'"

"Quite right, and I am the owner of the *Rajah*. Your husband has just bought that little bit of property down the bay; the one with a cottage and a flag pole, you know."

"What are you talking about, sir? My husband is hundreds and hundreds of miles away at sea."

"Oh, no, madam, it's you who are at sea. Of course, he didn't buy the property personally. I have acted as his agent, and I come merely to tell you of the transaction. The deeds are promised by noon to-morrow, when I am promising myself the pleasure of handing them to you."

"Then his venture has turned out a success? I had my doubts of it."

"So had I, madam, but we who predict disaster are often confounded. Everything is all right, as you remark." Then, turning to the one who had let him in, he said reproachfully: "Please don't scowl at me like that, but close the door and invite me into the parlor. Don't you see I'm a visitor?"

The girl said nothing, but looked at her mother.

"Come this way, sir," said the woman, opening the door at the left, whereupon the girl, with visible reluctance, closed the front door.

"Where are the other two girls'?" demanded Stranleigh.

"They are in the kitchen, sir."

"Please send for them. I wish to see the whole family, being so well acquainted with the captain."

The still unmollified door opener, at a nod from her mother, disappeared, returning shortly with the two younger children shrinking bashfully behind their elder sister, who quite evidently ruled the household.

"Ah," said Stranleigh, "what a fine family! It is evident that these girls did not depend for their beauty solely on their father."

"I think," said the elder girl haughtily, "that my father is the finest looking man in the world."

"You'll change your mind some of these days, miss, or I'm greatly mistaken. I admit the worth of your father, but you'll never see his picture on a beauty post card. And now, if you're prepared for a bit of news, and if every one promises not to faint, I'll tell you what it is."

"Oh, he isn't arrested?" cried the wife in alarm.

"Arrested? Of course not. Why should he be? He is coaling my yacht at this moment somewhere in Southampton harbor, within half a mile of where you are sitting."

There were some shrieks of surprise at this intelligence, but Stranleigh went on unheeding.

"Now, as I have told you, the cottage is yours, and I wish you to do something very enterprising; to hustle, as they say in America. My motor boat is down at the landing, and can take you to and from the cottage as often as you like, and it will be speedier than tram or cab or railway carriage. Missus, you will be chief of the finest burst of shopping Southampton has ever seen. Your husband will land at the cottage at six o'clock tomorrow night. The chances are that the empty house will not be any the worse for a little cleaning, so your eldest daughter here should take with her a host of charwomen, and scrub the edifice from top room to basement. Then, madam, you are to go to whatever furniture shop you choose, ignore all that you now possess, and furnish every room in that house before four o'clock tomorrow."

"But, sir, that will cost a mint of money, and we——"

"Yes, I didn't expect it done for nothing, and I haven't the remotest idea what the total will be. But here are three hundred pounds to go on with. I got this purposely to-day in crisp Bank of England notes. Whatever more is needed I will pay you to-morrow."

"But how are we ever to pay you, sir?" asked the astonished woman.

"No need of that, madam. Your husband did me a very great service, and I am merely arranging this as a pleasant surprise for him, and also because of the intense admiration your eldest daughter exhibits for me."

The girl tossed her head.

"He's a humbug, mother; don't believe him. There's something bogus in all this. I'll warrant you those notes are counterfeit. He wants to get us out of the house, and then steal the furniture. I read about a person like him in the papers. He got seven years."

Lord Stranleigh laughed.

"Why, how sharp you are, unbelieving creature. You've guessed it the first time. Is the furniture in this villa worth three hundred pounds?"

"No, it isn't," said the girl promptly.

"Very well. Take those notes to the bank, and get golden sovereigns for them, leaving your mother on guard till you return. They'll probably ask you where you got them, and you will answer thus: 'They are the proceeds of a draft for three hundred pounds which Lord Stranleigh of Wychwood cashed at the London and County to-day, at half-past eleven.' If they still wish to know how you came by them, say that Lord Stranleigh is the owner of several steamships, and that your father is captain of the largest of them. Say nothing of the *Rajah*, because he is now chief of a steamer twice her size. I took notes because they were lighter to carry, but when you get the gold I hope you will do what I ask of you, and leave this house promptly, so that I can steal its furniture without molestation."

"Are you Lord Stranleigh?" gasped the mother.

"Yes, madam, and there's one other favor I beg of you, and of these three charming girls. Mention to nobody that your father has returned. Neither he nor I wish this known for a while yet, and I am quite sure four women can keep the secret, even if one man can't."

"There's nothing wrong, is there?" asked the anxious woman.

"Nothing wrong at all. It's merely a matter concerning his new ship, which lies at Plymouth, where he must go on the morning of day after tomorrow."

Energetic as the captain's family was, they never put in such a day and a half of nervous, capable speed in their lives before, and this included the intervening night, during which none of them slept.

By five o'clock in the afternoon everything was ship-shape, although not quite to the satisfaction of the eldest daughter, and at six Lord Stranleigh had the felicity of introducing the captain to his possessions, human and material, old and new. Then he rushed back in his motor boat, and took the train to London.

CHAPTER VIII—THE "RAJAH" GETS INTO LEGAL DIFFICULTIES

ACAB from the London terminus speedily deposited Lord Stranleigh at his favorite club in Pall Mall. Two acquaintances coming down the steps nodded to him casually, so casually that the salutation, taken in conjunction with the lack of all interest displayed in the smoking room when he entered, caused him to realize that he had never been missed, and this indifference keeps a man from becoming too conceited when he has victoriously pitted his intelligence against bears or brigands in far-away corners of the earth, and lives to tell the tale, or keep quiet about it, as the case may be. As he was attired in the ordinary business suit that had done two days' hard duty at Southampton, he could not commit the solecism of entering the dining room. Indeed, gleaming, snowy shirt fronts were so prevalent in the smoking room itself that he experienced the unaccustomed, but rather enjoyable feeling of being a wild and woolly pioneer, who had strayed by mistake into a stronghold of fashionable civilization. The dining room being forbidden ground, Stranleigh contented himself with a couple of sandwiches and a tankard of German beer. As he partook of this frugal fare, a broad shirt front bore down upon him that reminded him of the sail of a racing yacht.

"Hello, Stranleigh," said Sir William Grainger, the owner of the shirt front. "Remember me telling you last week that Flying Scud was sure of a place in the Maple-Durham stakes?"

"I don't remember having received that information from you," replied Stranleigh. "Did Flying Scud pull it off, then?"

"Pull it off? Why, the race isn't run till tomorrow."

"Oh, I beg pardon, I had forgotten the date."

"Well, Stranleigh, I've got it straight that Flying Scud will romp in a winner. It's a sure thing. Don't you give it away, but act on the hint, and you won't be sorry. Odds are twenty-five to one at the present moment, and for every blooming quid you put up, you'll get a pony."

"That's very attractive, Billy."

"Attractive? Why, it's simply found money."

"Ah, well, such chances are not for me, Billy. I've had to pawn my evening togs in order to get a sandwich and a glass of beer. I'm a hornyhanded son of toil trying to pick up an honest living. Why don't you follow my example, Billy, and do something useful? This deplorable habit of betting on the races will lead you into financial straits by and by, and what is worse, the gambling fever may become chronic if you don't check it in time."

Sir William Grainger laughed joyously at this. He was a young man who had already run through a large patrimony left him by his father, and since that time had developed a genius for borrowing which would have done credit to Harriman, the railway king.

"Come, Stranleigh, don't preach, or at least, if you do preach, don't hedge. You know what I want. Lend me a pony till next Monday, there's a good fellow. That sum will bring me in six hundred and twenty-five pounds before to-morrow night. I've figured it all out on a sheet of club paper, but I'm stony broke, so fork over the twenty-five, Stranleigh."

Lord Stranleigh, without demur, took from his pocketbook some Bank of England notes of ten pounds each, selected three of them, and passed them on to Sir William, who thus getting five pounds more than he had asked for, lovingly fingered the tenacious, crisp pieces of paper, then put forward a bluff of getting one of them changed, that he might return the extra money.

"Oh, don't trouble about that," said Stranleigh, somewhat wearily. He had had a tiring day at Southampton, and beer and sandwiches were not a very inspiring meal at the end of it. "Don't trouble about that. If you take another sheet of club paper, you may be able to calculate how much more the extra five pounds will bring you in to-morrow night."

"By Jove, that's true," said Sir William, much relieved, and then the ease with which he had made the haul seemed to stir up his covetousness and still further submerge all self-respect.

"Talking of the extra amount I will gain reminds me, Stranleigh, that if you will give me one more ten-pound note, the whole loot will be an even thousand at twenty-five to one, you know. I'll pay it all back on Monday, but it seems a pity to miss such a chance, doesn't it?"

"How wonderfully you can estimate the odds, Billy. If forty pounds will bring you a thousand, then, as you say, it would be a pity to miss such an opportunity. Well, here you are," and he passed the fourth ten-pound note into the other's custody.

Still Sir William lingered. Perhaps it would have been more merciful if his lordship had demurred rather strenuously against accommodating him with the so-called loan. The sight of the other's notes now returning to his pocket filled him with envy. He felt some remnant of reluctance in attempting to increase his acquisition, so he put it in another form:

"I say, Stranleigh, if you'd like me to lay a bit on for you, so far as Flying Scud is concerned, I'll do it with pleasure."

"Thanks, old man, but I shan't trouble you. I intend to put on some money, but it will be against Flying Scud."

"What! have you heard anything?" cried Sir William in alarm, but the other interrupted——

"I know nothing about the horse at all, but I know a good deal about your luck, and I'll have that forty pounds back on Monday, without troubling you, except by betting against you." Sir William laughed a little, shrugged his shoulders, and walked away with the loot.

"Yes," murmured Stranleigh to himself, "this is dear old London again, sure enough. The borrowing of money has begun."

In spite of being touched for varying amounts, Lord Stranleigh enjoyed to the full his return to the Metropolis, and for many days strolled down Piccadilly with the easy grace of a man about town, the envy of less fortunate people who knew him. This period of indolence was put an end to by the receipt of a telegram from Mackeller. That capable young man had sent his message from the northwest corner of Brittany, having ordered the *Rajah* to be run into the roadstead of Brest. The communication informed Stranleigh that Mackeller had hoisted up a portion of the cargo, and placed it aboard a lugger, which was to sail direct for Portreath. This transhipment of part of the cargo had brought Plimsoll's mark on the side of the *Rajah* into view once more, and the steamer might now enter the harbor of Plymouth without danger of being haled before the authorities, charged with overloading. He expected to reach Plymouth next day.

Stranleigh was lunching at home that day because in the morning he had been favored with a telephone call, and on putting the receiver to his ear, had distinguished the still, small voice of Conrad Schwartzbrod, who appeared to be trying to say something with reference to the *Rajah*. Stranleigh was afflicted with a certain dislike of the telephone, and often manifested an impatience with its working which he did not usually show when confronted with the greater evils of life, so after telling the good Mr. Schwartzbrod to stand farther away from the transmitter, to come closer, to speak louder, he at last admitted he could not understand what was being said, and invited the financier to call upon him at his house that afternoon at half past two, if what he had to say was important enough to justify a journey from the city to the West End.

At the luncheon table Mackeller's long telegram was handed to him, and, after he had read it, Stranleigh smiled as he thought how nearly its arrival had coincided with Schwartzbrod's visit, and he wondered how much the latter would give for its perusal if he knew of its existence. He surmised that the Stock Exchange magnate was becoming a little anxious because of the nonarrival of the *Rajah* at Lisbon, where, doubtless, his emissaries awaited her. In spite of his pretense of misapprehension, he had heard quite distinctly at the telephone receiver that Schwartz-brod had just learned he was the owner of the *Rajah*, and that he wished to renew his charter of that slow-going, deliberate steam vessel, but he could not deny himself the pleasure of crossquestioning so crafty an opponent face to face. He had been expecting an application from Conrad Schwartzbrod for some days, and now it had arrived almost too late, for he directed Ponderby to secure him a berth on the Plymouth express for that night.

The young nobleman did not receive the elderly capitalist in his business office downstairs, as perhaps would have been the more suitable, but greeted him instead in the ample and luxurious drawing-room on the first floor, where Stranleigh, enjoying the liberty of a bachelor, was smoking an after-luncheon cigar, and he began the interview by offering a similar one to his visitor, which was declined. Mr. Schwartzbrod, it seemed, never smoked.

The furtive old man was palpably nervous and ill at ease. He sat on the extreme edge of an elegant chair, and appeared not to know exactly what to do with his hands. The news which had reached him from Sparling & Bilge in Southampton, that Lord Stranleigh was the new owner of the *Rajah*, had disquieted Schwartzbrod, and his manner showed this to his indolent host, who lounged back in an easy-chair, calmly viewing the newcomer with an expression of countenance that was almost cherublike in its innocence.

"'You miss a great deal of pleasure in life.'"

"Sorry you don't smoke," drawled the younger man. "You miss a great deal of pleasure in life by your abstention."

"It is a habit I never acquired, my lord, and so perhaps I do not feel the lack of it so much as one accustomed to tobacco might suppose. I lead a very busy life, and, indeed, a somewhat anxious one, since times are so bad in the city, therefore I have little opportunity of cultivating what I might call—I hope with no offense—the smaller vices."

"Ah, there speaks a large trader. You go in for the big things in life, whether in finance or in vice."

"I hope I may say without vanity, my lord, that I have always avoided vice, large or small."

"Lucky man; I wish I could make the same confession. So times are bad in the city, are they?"

"Yes, they are."

"Then why don't you chuck the city, and come and live in the West End where life is easy?"

"A rich man may live where he pleases, my lord, but I have been a hard worker all my life."

"Poor, but honest, eh? Still, when all's said and done, Mr. Schwartzbrod, I really believe that you hard workers enjoy your money better when you get it than we leisurely people who have never known the lack of it. I believe in honesty myself, and if I were not of so indolent a nature, I think I might perhaps have become an honest man. But a busy laborer like yourself, Mr. Schwartzbrod, has not come to the West End to hear me talk platitudes about honesty. In America the man goes West who intends to work hard. In London a man comes west when he has made money.

"'You miss a great deal of pleasure in life.'"

"He has his pile in the city, and expects to cease work. You have come west temporarily to see me about some matter which the telephone delighted in mixing up with buzzings and rattlings and intermittent chattering that made your theme difficult to comprehend. Perhaps you will be good enough to let me know in what way I may serve you."

"At the time when I expected to operate the gold field, which you know of, my lord, I chartered a steamer, named the *Rajah*, at Southampton."

"Oh, the *Rajah!*" interrupted his lordship, sitting up, a gleam of intelligent comprehension animating his face. "The *Rajah* was what you were trying to say? I thought you were speaking of a Jolly Roger. Roger was the word that came over to me, and 'Jolly Roger' means the flag of a pirate ship, or something pertaining to piracy, so I, recognizing your voice, thinks to myself: 'What, in the name of Moses and the Prophets, can a respectable city personage mean by speaking of the Jolly Roger, as if he were a captain of buccaneers.' Oh, yes, the *Rajah! Now* I understand. Proceed, Mr. Schwartzbrod."

The personage seemed to turn a trifle more sallow than usual as the other went on enthusiastically talking of pirate ships and buccaneers, but he surmised that the young nobleman meant nothing in particular, as he sank back once more in his easy-chair, and again half closed his eyes, blowing the smoke of his cigar airily aloft. Presently, moistening his lips, Conrad Schwartzbrod found voice, convinced that the other's allusion to marine pillage was a mere coincidence, and not a covert reference to Frowningshield and his merry men, or to the mission of the *Rajah* herself.

"I was about to say, my lord, that I had chartered the *Rajah* from a firm of shipping people in Southampton, intending to use her in the development of the mineral property in West Africa. That property having passed from the hands of myself and my associates into yours, my lord, I determined to employ the *Rajah* in the South American cattle trade, as we own an extensive tract of territory in the Argentine, the interests of which we are endeavoring to forward with the ultimate object of floating a company."

Again the prospective company promoter moistened his lips when they had safely delivered this interesting piece of fiction.

"So the *Rajah* has gone to the Argentine Republic, has she?" said Stranleigh.

"Yes, my lord."

"Filled with dynamite and mining machinery, eh? Surely a remarkable cargo for a herdsman to transport, Mr. Schwartzbrod?"

"Well, you see, my lord, the dynamite and machinery was on our hands, and as there are many mines in South America, we thought we could sell the cargo there to better advantage than in Southampton."

"Of course I don't in the least doubt, Mr. Schwartzbrod, that you own large ranches in South America, but I strongly suspect— —"

He paused, and opened his eyes to half width, looking quizzically at his *vis-à-vis*.

"You strongly suspect what, my lord?" muttered Schwartzbrod.

"I suspect that you own a mine in South America that you are keeping very quiet about."

"Well, my lord," confessed Schwartzbrod, with apparent diffidence, "it is rarely wise to speak of these things prematurely."

"That is quite true, and I have really no wish to pry into your secrets, but to tell the truth, I felt a little sore about your action with regard to the *Rajah*."

"My action? What action?"

"You must admit, Mr. Schwartzbrod, that when I acquired those so-called gold fields, I became possessor of everything the company owned, or at least I thought I did. Now, in the company was vested the charter of the *Rajah*, and it was the company's money which bought all the materials with which you have sailed away to South America. It therefore seemed to me—I don't wish to put it harshly—that you had, practically, made off with a portion of my property."

"You astonish me, my lord. It never occurred to me that such a view could be held by any one, especially one like yourself, so well acquainted with facts."

Stranleigh shrugged his shoulders.

"Acquainted with the facts? Oh, I don't know that I'm so very well versed in them. I'm not a business man, Mr. Schwartzbrod, and although I engage business men to look after my interests, it seems to me that sometimes they are not as sharp as they might be. I thought, after the acquisition of the company's property, that the charter of the *Rajah* and the contents of her hold belonged to me, just as much as the company's money in the bank did, or as its gold in West Africa."

"I assure you, my lord, you are mistaken. The *Rajah* and her charter were not mentioned in the documents of agreement between you and me, while the money in the bank was. But aside from all that, my lord, you gave me a document covering all that had been done previous to its signing, and the *Rajah* had sailed from South America several days before that instrument was completed. Everything was done legally, and under the advice of competent solicitors—yours and mine."

"Do not mistake me, Mr. Schwartzbrod; I am not complaining at all, nor even doubting the legality of the documents to which you refer. I am merely saying that I thought the *Rajah* and her cargo was to be turned over to me. There, doubtless, I was mistaken. It seems to me after all, Mr. Schwartzbrod, that there is a higher criterion of action than mere legality. You, probably, would be the first to admit that there is such a thing as moral right which may not happen to coincide with legal right."

"Assuredly, assuredly, my lord. I should be very sorry indeed to infringe upon any moral law, but, unfortunately, in this defective world, my lord, experience has shown that it is always well to set down in plain black and white exactly what a man means when a transfer is made, otherwise your remembrance of what was intended may differ entirely from mine, and yet each of us may be scrupulously honest in our contention."

"Yes, you have me there, Mr. Schwartzbrod. I see the force of your reasoning, and a man has only himself to blame if he neglects those necessary precautions which you have mentioned, so we will say nothing more about that phase of the matter, but you will easily understand that having thought myself entitled to the use of the Rajah, I may not feel myself inclined to renew your charter now."

"Ah, there again, my lord, it is all set down in black and white. The charter distinctly states that I am to have the option of renewal for a further three months when the first three months has expired."

"You corner me at every point of the game, Mr. Schwartzbrod. I take it, then, that my purchase of the *Rajah* does not invalidate the arrangement made with you by her former owners?"

"Certainly not, my lord. If you buy a property, you take over all its liabilities."

"That seems just and reasonable. So your application for renewal is a mere formality, against which any objection of mine would be futile?"

"Did not Sparling & Bilge explain to you, my lord, that the steamer was under charter?"

"I never saw those estimable gentlemen, Mr. Schwartzbrod. The purchase was made by an agent of mine, and I have no doubt Sparling & Bilge made him acquainted with all the liabilities I was acquiring. If you insist on exercising your option, Mr. Schwartzbrod, I suppose I must either postpone the development of my gold-bearing property, or charter another steamer?"

"I should be sorry to put you to the trouble and expense of chartering another boat when the *Rajah* is so well suited to your purpose, my lord. It is possible that, even before the first charter is completed, the *Rajah* may have returned to Southampton, and our experiments in the cattle trade may end with the first voyage. In that case I shall be very pleased to relinquish my claim upon your steamer."

"That is very good of you, Mr. Schwartzbrod. By the way, where is the *Rajah* now?"

"She is probably in some port along the Argentine coast, south of Buenos Ayres."

"Really? Then perhaps you can tell me where Mackeller is?"

"Mackeller? You mean the mining engineer, son of the stockbroker?"

"Yes, I thought he was in my employment, and sent him down to attend the loading of the *Rajah*, but he has disappeared. Did you engage him?"

"No, I know nothing of him."

"I thought perhaps he had sailed with the *Rajah*."

"Not to my knowledge. Doesn't his father know where he is?"

"His father appears to know no more than I do. Just as much, or just as little, whichever way you like to put it."

"He's no employee of mine, my lord."

"I think he should have given me notice if he intended to quit my service. Probably he has gone hunting a gold mine for himself."

"I think there are many mining engineers more valuable than young Mackeller, my lord. He always seemed to me a stubborn, unmannerly person."

"Yes, he lacked the polish which the city gives to a man. I suppose his life in the various wildernesses he has visited has not been conducive to the acquirement of the art of politeness. Still, as you say, there is no lack of mining engineers in London, and doubtless, when the time comes that I need one, I shall find a suitable man for the vacancy."

"I shall be very glad to help you in the selection, my lord, if you care to consult me."

"Thanks, I'll remember that. I take it with regard to this charter that I have to sign something, haven't I, although I suppose I shouldn't sign until my solicitors are consulted; still, I feel quite safe in your hands, Mr. Schwartzbrod, and if you will send me the document, and mark with a lead pencil where my signature is to go, I shall attend to it."

"I have brought the papers with me, my lord," said the financier eagerly, extracting them from his pocket.

"Could you also oblige me with a fountain pen? Ah, thanks. You go about fully equipped for business, Mr. Schwartzbrod. That's what it is to be a methodical man."

His lordship cleared a little space on the table, and wrote his name at the bottom of two documents, which, however, he took the precaution to read with some care before attaching his autograph to them, in spite of his disclaimer that he understood nothing about these things. He complained languidly of the obscure nature of the papers, and said it was no wonder lawyers were so much needed to elucidate them. Schwartzbrod put the papers in his pocket with a satisfaction he could scarcely conceal, then, standing up, he buttoned his coat, ever so much more alert than the weary young man, half his age, who stood up from his writing as if the exertion had almost exhausted him. He, however, made a quiet, casual remark in parting that suddenly electrified the room and made his guest shiver and turn pale.

"When did you say you expected the *Rajah* from Lisbon, Mr. Schwartzbrod?"

For a few moments there was intense stillness. Stranleigh was lighting another cigar, and did not look up at the terror-stricken man, whose bulging eyes were filled with fear.

"Lisbon—Lisbon?" he gasped, trying to secure control of his features. "I—I never mentioned Lisbon."

"Oh, yes, you did. You said she was at some point south of Lisbon, didn't you?"

"I said Buenos Ayres."

Stranleigh made a gesture of impatience as if he were annoyed with himself.

"Why, of course you said Buenos Ayres. How stupid of me. I am always mixing these foreign places up. I suppose it is because the Argentine Republic is one of those former Spanish possessions, and Lisbon being in Spain, I confused the two."

"Lisbon is in Portugal, my lord; the capital of Portugal."

"You are right. It was Madrid I was thinking of Madrid is in Spain, isn't it?"

"Yes, my lord."

"And it isn't a port, either?"

"No, my lord."

"And is Lisbon on the sea?"

"On the river Tagus, my lord."

"I am an ignoramus, that's what I am. I ought really to go to school again. I have forgotten everything I learned there. Well, good afternoon, Mr. Schwartzbrod. Anything else I can do for you, you know, don't hesitate to call on me. We financiers must stand by one another, while times are so bad in the city."

The young man stood at the head of the stairs, a cigar between his lips, and his hands deep in his trousers pockets, seeing which Mr. Schwartzbrod, who had tentatively made a motion to shake hands in farewell, thought better of it, and went down the stairs, at the bottom of which the silent Ponderby waited to open the door for him. When he reached the floor below Schwartzbrod cast one look over his shoulder up the stairs. The young man still stood on the landing, gazing contemplatively down upon his parting guest. He nodded pleasantly, and "Ta-ta," he said, but the expression on Schwartzbrod's face could not have shown greater perturbation if Satan himself had occupied Stranleigh's place.

"A very uncomfortable companion is an uneasy conscience, even in the city," said Stran-leigh to himself, as he turned away.

Schwartzbrod hailed a cab, and drove to his office in the city; anxious about the *Rajah*; glad he had secured the renewal of the charter without protest or investigation; uneasy regarding Stranleigh's apparently purposeless remarks about pirates and Lisbon. Arriving at his office, he rang for his confidential clerk.

"Any word from Lisbon?" he demanded.

"Yes, sir. The same code word. No sign of the *Rajah* there, sir."

"How long is it since you sent warning to all our agents along the Atlantic coast and the Mediterranean to look out for her?"

"Just a week to-day, sir, and a wire came in shortly after you left, from our man at Brest. I'd have telephoned you, sir, if I had known where you had gone."

"Give it to me, give it to me, give it to me," repeated Schwartzbrod impatiently. He clutched it in his trembling hands, and read:

"Steamer flying English flag, named *Rajah* Wilkie captain, in roadstead to-day. Unloading ore into lugger."

The moral Mr. Schwartzbrod now gave way to a paroxysm of bitter language that was dreadful to hear, but his stolid clerk seemed used to it, and bent his head before the storm. During a lull for lack of breath he ventured one remark:

"It can't be our ship, sir. Our man is Captain Simmons."

"What has that to do with it, you fool?" roared Schwartzbrod. "That old scoundrel Simmons can easily change his name. He's sold me out, the sanctimonious hound. Very likely he and Frowningshield are both in the plot against me. Simmons is a thief, for all his canting objections when we were striking a bargain. I don't believe Frowningshield's any better, and he's got more brains. They'll smelt the ore in France, after carrying it to some suitable spot along the coast in sailing boats. But it'll take two or three days to unload, and I'll give old Simmons a fright before that is done. See if there's a steamer from Southampton to St. Malo to-night. If not I must go to Brest by way of Paris. I can't trust this job to any one else."

As it happened there was a boat that evening for St. Malo, and so the two persons who had indulged in a long conversation regarding the *Rajah* that afternoon were each in pursuit of her, moving westward; Schwartzbrod in his berth on board the St. Malo boat, Stranleigh in his berth on the Plymouth express, while between the two the stanch old *Rajah* was threshing her way across the Channel between Brest and Plymouth, heading for the latter seaport.

Next day Stranleigh greeted Mackeller with something almost approaching enthusiasm. Neither of them entertained the least suspicion that the stop at Brest might put Conrad on the trail; but even if they had, they must have known that the arrival of the *Rajah* at Plymouth would have entailed similar consequences if Schwartzbrod's minions were looking sharply after his interests.

The *Rajah's* stay at Plymouth was very short, merely giving time for the crew of the yacht to take its station aboard the *Rajah*, under command of Captain Wilkie, while the crew that had brought the *Rajah* into port was placed in the care of Captain Simmons, whose big steamer, the *Wychwood,* was not yet ready to sail. The *Rajah* then rounded the southwest corner of England, and found a berth in the little haven of Portreath, within easy distance of the smelting furnace. The *Rajah* was unloaded with the utmost speed, and the ore conveyed as quickly as possible to the inclosure which surrounded the smelting furnace. Stranleigh thought it just as well to get his raw material under cover with the least possible delay, for, although Portreath was not a tourist center, one could never be quite certain that some scientific chap might not happen along, who, picking up a specimen, would know that it contained gold and not copper. Besides this, the engineer of the *Rajah* reported certain defects in engines and boilers that needed to be seen to and amended before it was safe to face so long a voyage again; therefore, that no time should be lost, the *Rajah* was hurried back to Plymouth to undergo the necessary repairs.

When, after its long abandonment, Lord Stranleigh, with the aid of Mackeller, restarted his ancient copper mine in Cornwall, he, knowing nothing of figures, as he said, turned over the mathematical department of the business to an accountant, one of the twelve business men who kept his affairs in order. Just before leaving London for Plymouth, he requested this accountant to furnish him with a statement of profit and loss, so far as the mine was concerned. This statement he merely glanced at, saw with satisfaction that the working had resulted in a deficit, and put the document into his pocket. When the *Rajah* left Plymouth to worry her way round the toe of England to Portreath, Lord Stranleigh and Mackeller took train from Plymouth, and reached Redruth in two hours and fifteen minutes, from which station they drove together to the copper mine, Stranleigh having given Mackeller the statement of profit and loss, and instructing him what he should say when he met the manager of the mine, whom Peter himself had installed in that position.

Arriving at the office of the works, Mackeller consulted with the manager, while Lord Stranleigh, beautifully attired in fine garments quite unsuitable for such a locality, strolled round, taking such intelligent interest in his environment as a casual tourist displays in unaccustomed surroundings. The grimy, hard-working smelters gazed with undisguised contempt at this dandified specimen of humanity, who had so unexpectedly wandered in among them, and made remarks on his personal appearance more distinguished for force than courtesy. To these uncomplimentary allusions the young man paid not the slightest attention, but dawdled about, one of the men complained, as if he owned the place. At last the manager and Mackeller came out of the office together, and word was sent down the pit that all the miners were to come up. Ribald comment ceased, and an uneasy feeling spread among the employees that something unpleasant was about to happen. Their intuition was justified when all the men were gathered together, and the manager began to speak. He informed them that the reopening of the mine had been merely an experiment, and he regretted to add that this experiment had failed through the simple elementary fact that the amount of copper produced cost more than it would fetch in the metal market of the world. Operations had been conducted at a loss, and the proprietor was thus reluctantly compelled to disband his forces, all except four smelters, who would remain to assist in converting into ingots the remnant of the ore which had been mined. This intelligence was received in doleful silence by those whom it affected. Each of them before now had faced the tragedy caused by lack of work, but custom had made its recurrence none the more welcome for all that.

The manager, after a pause, continued. The proprietor, he said, was Lord Stranleigh, and he had given orders which, for generosity, the manager in all his experience thought was unexampled. Each man was to receive a year's pay. At this announcement the gloom suddenly lifted, and a resounding cheer went up from the men. The manager added that he himself had been given an important position in one of his lordship's coal mines in the north, whereupon the good-natured crowd cheered the manager, who appeared to be popular with them.

"And now," concluded the manager, "as Lord Stranleigh is himself present, he will perhaps choose from the six smelters the four whom he wishes to employ."

Stranleigh had been standing apart from the group, listening to the eloquence of the manager, and now every one turned and looked at him with more than ordinary interest. His hands, as usual, were in his pockets, a cigarette between his lips, which nevertheless did not conceal the humorous smile with which his lordship regarded the six smelters, who were quite evidently panic-stricken to learn that they had been exercising their robustious wit on the man with the money; the important boss who paid the wage. Lord Stranleigh slowly removed his left hand from his pocket, and took the cigarette from between his lips.

"I think, Mr. Manager," he said, "we will retain all six," and so the congregation was dismissed.

The hoisting gang was retained until all tools and movable ore were hoisted from the bottom of the mine to the surface of the earth. Stranleigh himself went down when the cage made its last trip, and there, by torchlight, examined the workings, listening to explanations by Mackeller. When he reached daylight again he ordered the dismantling of the hoisting apparatus, which work of destruction was taken to mean the final abandonment of the copper mine. Mackeller, thrifty person, protested against this demolition.

Stranleigh smiled, but did not countermand the order. He and Mackeller took up their quarters in the manager's house, its late occupant having taken his departure for the north. The six smelters were rude, unintelligent, uneducated men, who saw no difference between one yellow bar and another, so there was little risk of discovery through their detection.

"What are you going to do with the gold ingots?" asked Mackeller.

"I was thinking of placing them in a safe deposit vault."

"You will need to look well to its locks, bolts, and bars," said the cautious engineer.

"There will be no bolts and bars," said Stranleigh. "I shall leave the ingots open to the sky, without lock or latch. Nobody will interfere with them."

"Bless my soul, you'll never be so foolish as that?" cried Mackeller. "Why, even the copper was protected by the strongest and safest locks I could secure."

Lord Stranleigh merely shrugged his shoulders, and made no further explanation of his intentions.

At the first smelting the gold was run into ingots weighing about a hundred pounds each. When the smelters had departed for the day, and the gates were closed, Stranleigh said to Mackeller:

"Come along, and I'll show you my safe deposit vault."

With this he hoisted to his shoulder one of the ingots; still warm, walked to the mouth of the pit, and flung it into space.

"Not a bad idea," growled Mackeller, as he followed the example of his chief, until between them all the gold from the first smelting rested on the deep and dark floor of the mine.

One day, as the two were sitting together consuming the frugal lunch that Peter had prepared, a telegram was brought in to Lord Stranleigh. The young man laughed when he read it, and tossed it across the table to Mackeller, who read:

"*Rajah* ready to sail, but to-day was taken possession of by legal authorities under action of a man named Schwartzbrod. I am under arrest charged with stealing the *Rajah*. No objection going to prison, but await instructions. Wilkie, captain."

"By Jove, the enemy has tracked her," ejaculated Peter. "I wonder how they did it!"

"That isn't the point to wonder over, Peter, when you remember that the arrival and departure of shipping is announced in every morning paper. The wonder is that they didn't get hold of her some days ago. Oh, dear me, how I am pestered by obstreperous men! Here are you constantly trying to involve me in a fight, and now here is Schwartzbrod entangling me in the meshes of the law, while, peaceful man that I am, I detest equally battles or lawsuits, but the righteous have always been persecuted, and I suppose I must accept my share of trouble. Nevertheless, I anticipate some amusement with my friend Schwartzbrod. If you don't help me, Peter, don't help the bear, and you'll see the funniest legal fight that ever happened."

With this Stranleigh retired to dress for town.

"Peter," he said, on emerging from his bedroom, attired as if he intended a dawdle down Piccadilly rather than a scramble over Cornish hills, "Peter, I am going to desert you. Continue the smelting as if we had not parted, and fling as many bars of gold down that pit as you can, thankful that for our purposes it is not bottomless, even though the possession of too much gold may lead to such. It is not that I like your cooking less, but that I love the cuisine of my club more."

"You are going to London, then?"

"Ultimately to London, my son, but first to Redruth station; then to Plymouth. I cannot allow my captain courageous to be flung into prison merely to please Conrad Schwartzbrod, who ought to be there himself. I must foregather at Plymouth with some one learned in the law, and so disconcert, delay, annoy, and at least partially beggar that old thief Schwartzbrod; therefore, ta-ta, my son, and be as good as you can during my absence, and when you feel proud because of your ever accumulating wealth, remember how difficult it is for a rich man to enter heaven, and thus resume your natural modesty. Good-by."

CHAPTER IX—THE FINAL FINANCIAL STRUGGLE WITH SCHWARTZBROD

ARRIVING at Redruth, Stranleigh sent off three telegrams, one instructing his chief solicitors in London to request the leading marine lawyer of Plymouth to call upon him at once at the Grand Hotel in that town. The second telegram bade Captain Wilkie cheer up, as ample bail was approaching him by the next train from the west, requesting him, if at liberty, to call at the Grand Hotel about six o'clock. The third telegram secured a suite of rooms at the Grand Hotel, and this task finished, Stranleigh had just time to catch the 2.49 train for Plymouth.

On driving up to the Grand Hotel shortly after six o'clock, he found both Captain Wilkie and Mr. Docketts, the marine lawyer, waiting for him, and the three went together up to the engaged apartments.

"So they haven't put you in quod, captain," said the young man, as he shook hands with him.

"No, sir; they thought better of that. In fact, there seems to be a good deal of hesitation about their procedure. They placed men in possession, and then have taken them out again. Just before I left the ship a fresh lot came aboard. At first they were going to put handcuffs on me, then they consulted about it, and asked if I could provide bail. Not knowing whether you wished me to go to prison or not, I refused to answer."

"Safest thing in the absence of instructions," put in Mr. Docketts. "What is it all about, my lord?"

"It's rather a complicated case, Mr. Docketts," said Stranleigh, throwing himself into the easiest chair he could find, "and it is not necessary to go into the whole story at the present time."

The lawyer shook his head doubtfully.

"If I am to be of any assistance, Lord Stranleigh, I think you should tell me everything. A point that may seem unimportant to the lay mind, often proves of the utmost significance to the legal student."

"You are wrong, Mr. Docketts. What you are thinking of is the detective story. It is the detective that the slightest incident furnishes with an important clew. You mustn't insult my intellect by calling it a lay mind, Mr. Docketts, because I take my marine law from that excellent practitioner, Clark Russell; therefore, when it comes to ships I know what I am talking about. The first point I wish to impress on you is that I am not to appear in this case. No one is to know who engages you. The second point is that no action will be fought in the courts. I could settle the case in ten minutes merely by going to the venerable Conrad Schwartzbrod, who has heedlessly set the law in action; but such a course on my part would be most unfair to an eminent limb of the law like yourself, who wishes to earn honest fees."

Mr. Docketts bowed rather gravely, an inclination of the head which contrived subtly to convey respect for his lordship's rank in life, and yet mild disapproval of his flippant utterances.

"I always advise my clients, my lord, to avoid litigation if they can."

"Quite right, Mr. Docketts. That is good legal etiquette, so long as the advice is conveyed in such a manner that it does not convince the client. Now this steamer, the *Rajah,* belongs to me, but it has been chartered for a number of months by the aforesaid Conrad Schwartzbrod—I trust I am using correct legal phraseology—and the aforesaid Conrad Schwartzbrod is one of the rankest, most unscrupulous scoundrels that the city of London has ever produced, which statement is regrettably libelous, but without prejudice, and uttered solely in the presence of friends. The law, of course, is designed to settle, briefly and inexpensively, such disputes as may be brought before it, nevertheless it is my wish that the law shall be twisted and turned from its proper purpose, so that this case may be dragged on as long as may be, with injunctions, and restraints, and cross pleas, and demurrers, and mandamuses, or any other damus things you can think of. Whenever you find you are cornered, Mr. Docketts, and must come into the light of day before a judge, you telegraph to me, and you will be astonished to know how speedily everything will be quashed."

Again the lawyer bowed very solemnly.

"I think I understand your lordship," he said impressively.

"I am sure of it, and I hope you will do me the pleasure of remembering your quickness of comprehension, so that you may charge extra for it when you send in the bill. I assure you, quite candidly, that nothing gives me such delight as the paying of an adequate fee to a competent man. If these people should attempt any further molestation of Captain Wilkie, you are to protect him, and I will furnish bail to any amount, reasonable or the reverse. And now, Mr. Docketts, if you will let me have your card, with your address on it, I shall leave the case in your hands."

Mr. Docketts complied with the request, and took his deferential departure. Captain Wilkie also rose, but Stranleigh waved him to his seat again.

"Sit you down, captain. Has the *Wychwood* sailed yet?"

"No, sir, she has not. I met Captain Simmons yesterday. He came across to the *Rajah* to take away some of his belongings that were still in his cabin. He said the Wychwood might be ready for sea to-morrow or next day."

"Well, I think I'll go over and call on him. I can do that before dinner. The estimable Mackeller has been my cook for some time past, and if this lucky action had not been begun by that public benefactor, Schwartzbrod, I do not know what would have become of me, for I did not wish to cast any reflection upon Mackeller's kitchen skill by desertion. But now that I have been compelled by law to desert him, I hope, captain, you will take pity on a lonesome man, and dine here with me at eight o'clock. I'll order such a dinner as will make this tavern sit up. You'll stand by, won't you, captain?"

"Thank you, sir, I'll be delighted."

"Well, that's settled. Now, if you will guide me to the *Wychwood*, I'll go aboard for a chat with Captain Simmons, and you will meet me in the dining room at eight o'clock."

The two parted alongside that huge steamer, the *Wychwood*, and Stranleigh climbed aboard, greeting Captain Simmons on deck.

"Well, captain, you haven't got off yet?"

"No, sir—my lord, not yet," said the astonished captain. "If you'd sent word you was coming, earl, I'd have had dinner prepared for you. As it is, there's nothing fit to eat aboard."

"I am accustomed to that, captain. I was just complaining to Wilkie, who brought me here, that Mackeller was my cook, and he seemed to sympathize. No, it's the other way about. You're coming to dine with me. I've invited Captain Wilkie, and we will form a hungry trio about a round table at the Grand Hotel to-night at eight. Three Plymouth brethren, as you may call us: you two practical salts, and me an amateur. Have you been back to that little cottage on Southampton water?"

"No, my lord—sir, but I keep a-thinking of it all the time with great pleasure, and the wife or one of the girls writes to me every day. They are delighted, sir—my lord. I didn't know till after you left that 'twas you had bought all that furniture, but you must let me pay for that, earl, on the instalment plan."

"Oh, that's all right, captain. You wait till I send round a collector. Never worry about payment till it's asked for. That's been my rule in life. Now, captain, take me down to your cabin. I wish to have a quiet chat with you, and on deck, with men about, is a little too public."

The captain led the way, and Stranleigh, standing, gazed about him.

"Ah, this is something like. This beats the *Rajah*, doesn't it?"

"Yes, it does, my lord—I mean sir. I never expected to find myself in a cabin like this, sir, and a fine ship she is, too; well found and stanch. I'd like to sail her into Southampton water some day, just to let the missus and the kids see her."

"I'll tell you what you must do, captain. Send a telegram to Mrs. Simmons and the girls, asking them to lock up the shop, and come at once to Plymouth. I'll make arrangements for them at the Grand Hotel and they'll stay here until you sail, which can't be for some days yet. And now to business, captain. Old Schwartzbrod has discovered where the *Rajah* is, and has jumped aboard with a blooming injunction or some such lawyer's devilment as that: tried to *habeas corpus* innocent old Wilkie, or whatever they call it;

anyhow, something that goes with handcuffs, but the old boy was game right through to the backbone, and was willing to go to the Bastile itself if his doing so would accommodate me, but I've invited him to dinner instead."

"Then Schwartzbrod will be trying to find me, very likely?" said Captain Simmons, in no way pleased with the prospect.

"I shouldn't wonder, so I'd keep my weather eye abeam, if I were you, for very likely Schwartzbrod is in Plymouth. Still, I've told an eminent lawyer to go full speed ahead, and I anticipate Schwartzbrod will have quite enough to occupy his mind in a few days. Now, Captain Simmons, although our acquaintance has been very short, I am going to trust you fully. Since this action was taken by Schwartzbrod, it has occurred to me that the proper person to go to the Paramakaboo River is the redoubtable captain who has already been there, and that person is yourself."

"Well; sir, Captain Wilkie has also been there, in your yacht, and perhaps he'd like this new ship. I'm sure he doesn't care about the *Rajah*."

"Oh, he doesn't need to care about the *Rajah*. He's off the *Rajah* for good, and will take command of my yacht again. No, you are the man for the Paramakaboo. You know Frowningshield, and you know his gang, and he knows you. Now, I leave everything to your own discretion. If you tell Frowningshield how everything stands, there is one chance in a thousand he may seize the *Wychwood,* and compel you to sail for Lisbon, or wherever he likes. It all depends how deeply he is in with that subtle rogue, Schwartzbrod."

"I'll tell him nothing about it, sir."

"That's my own advice. I should say nothing except that they have furnished you with a larger steamer, so that you can get away with double the quantity of ore, all of which is true enough. But if circumstances over which you have no control compel you to divulge the true state of affairs, get Frowningshield alone here in the cabin, and talk to him as I talked to you on the high seas. He's engaged in a criminal business, whether he is under the jurisdiction of the British flag or not; but the main point I wish you to impress upon him is this: I shall stand in Schwartzbrod's place; that is to say,

I shall make good to him, as I made good to you, every promise that rascal has given. I know that virtue is its own reward, yet I sometimes wish that virtue would oftener deal in the coin of the realm in addition. It doesn't seem fair that all the big compensations are usually on the devil's side. Anyhow, I trust this ship and this business entirely to you. You act as you think best, and if they compel you to sail to Lisbon or anywhere else, telegraph fully to me whenever you get into touch with a wire. I don't anticipate any trouble of that kind, however. Frowningshield will know on which side his bread is buttered, even if he is a villain, which I don't believe. Now, Schwartzbrod promised you five thousand pounds extra for three trips to Lisbon, and two thousand pounds for every additional voyage. How many additional voyages could you have made?"

"I couldn't have made one, sir, with the *Rajah*."

"Well, let us call it two. That amounts to nine thousand pounds. I'll give you a check for that amount to-morrow, and you can hand it to the missus to put in the bank when she returns to Southampton."

"I couldn't think of taking that from you, sir," said the captain, with an unfeigned look of distress.

"It's not from me at all, Captain Simmons. I am going to make Schwartzbrod hand over that amount to my bank. I am merely anticipating his payments; passing it on from him to you, as it were. In a similar way I shall recompense Frowningshield, and I shall give you a sufficient number of gold sovereigns with which to pay all his men, and this will create a certain satisfaction in the camp, even although there is no spot within a thousand miles where they can spend a penny. So, captain, you will load up your ship with an ample supply of provisions for those in camp, and take out to them anything that you think they may need, charging the same to me, which account I shall pass on to Schwartzbrod."

"But isn't there a chance, sir, that Schwartzbrod may charter another steamer, in which case we may have to fight?"

"No, I don't think so. I am having old Schwartzbrod watched, and from the latest report he has not even chartered a rowboat. No, I have extended his charter of the *Rajah* for an extra three months, and he will hope to get possession of her. It will take him a few days to realize the extent of the law's delay, and with such a start, together with the speed of the *Wychwood* you will find no difficulty about filling this ship, and getting away without encountering any opposition. No, I don't want any fight. You see, I can't spare Mackeller, and it would break his heart to think there was a ruction and he not in it.

"Here is a suggestion which has just occurred to me, and you may act on it or not as circumstances out there dictate. When the *Wychwood* is fully loaded with ore, and ready to sail, you might ask Frowningshield to come aboard with you for that twelve-mile run down the river. The steam launch could follow and take him back. Inform him that you have something important to say which cannot be told ashore, then get him down here into your cabin, and relate to him everything that has happened. He cannot stop the *Wychwood* then if he wanted to. Your crew will obey you, and no matter what commands he gave them to put about, they would pay no attention to him. Show him that he can make more money by being honest than by following the lead of old Schwartzbrod. Tell him you have received your nine thousand pounds—and, by the way, that reminds me I had better give you the check tonight before dinner, so that you can post it to your bank at Southampton, and receive the bank's receipt for it before you sail. The deposit receipt will be just as cheering to Mrs. Simmons as the check would be—and then you can tell Frowningshield, quite conscientiously, that the money is already in your hands. I always believe in telling the truth to a pirate like Frowningshield if it is at all possible. Don't imagine I'm preaching, captain. What I mean is that the truth is ever so much more convincing than even the cleverest of lies. We will suppose, then, that Frowningshield comes to the same decision that you did, and agrees to join me in preserving my own property from an unscrupulous thief. In that case tell him that Schwartzbrod will very likely send some other steamer to carry away the ore, as soon as he realizes he cannot again get hold of the *Rajah*, and that I shall expect Frowningshield and his merry men not to allow such a vessel to take away any of my ore."

"Shall I tell him to sink Schwartzbrod's steamer?"

"Sink her? No, bless my soul, no. What would you sink her for? Tell him to use gentle persuasion, and not give up the ore. An ordinary crew cannot fill the hold with ore which a hundred and fifty men refuse to allow them to touch. You don't need to fight. If Frowningshield will just line up his hundred and fifty men along that reef, one glance at their interesting faces will convince any ship's captain that he'd be safer out at sea.

"I think the *Wychwood* will answer our purposes very well. She is large and fast. Try to find out, if you can, exactly what Schwartzbrod promised Frowningshield and his men, and let me know when you return. Now, captain, I think you understand pretty well what your new duties are, so get off for the south just as quickly as you can. Meanwhile we must be moving on toward the Grand Hotel. I'm rather anxious to meet that dinner, and on the way we will send a telegram to Mrs. Simmons and the family. After that we three roisterers will make a night of it, for I must go up to London tomorrow."

Mackeller worked industriously at his smelting, dumping the gold down into the abandoned mine after his assistants had left him for the night. He was anxious to hear what had become of the *Rajah,* and what had happened to Captain Wilkie threatened with imprisonment, but no letter came from Lord Stranleigh, which was not to be wondered at, for all Stranleigh's friends knew his dislike of writing.

The third morning after Stranleigh's departure Mackeller received a long telegram which had evidently been handed in at London the night before. At first Mackeller thought it was in cipher, but a close study of the message persuaded him that no code was necessary for its disentanglement. It ran as follows:

"Take half a pound of butter, one pound of flour, half a pound of moist sugar, two eggs, one teaspoonful of essence of lemon, one fourth glass of brandy or sherry. Rub the butter, flour, and sugar well together, mix in the eggs after beating them, add the essence of lemon and the brandy. Drop the cakes upon a frying pan, and bake for half an hour in a quick oven."

Mackeller muttered some strenuous remarks to himself as at last he gathered in the purport of this communication. He detained the telegraph boy long enough to write a line which he sent to Lord Stranleigh's residence at a cost of sixpence.

"What have you done about the *Rajah*—Mackeller."

Late in the afternoon the telegraph boy returned, and bestowed upon the impatient and now irascible Mackeller the following instructions:

"For two persons alone at the mouth of a pit take one plump fowl, add white pepper and salt to suit the taste, one half spoonful of grated nutmeg, one half spoonful of pounded mace, a few slices of ham, three hard-boiled eggs, sliced thin, half a pint of water, and some puff paste crust to cover. Stew for half an hour, and when done strain off the liquor for gravy. Put a layer of fowl at the bottom of a pie dish, then a layer of ham, then the slices of hard-boiled egg, with the mace, nutmeg, pepper and salt between the layers. Put in half a pint of water, cover with puff paste, and bake for an hour and a half."

"I suppose," growled Mackeller to himself, "he thinks that's funny, but it will cost him a pretty penny if he keeps it up every day."

"Any answer?" said the telegraph boy.

"Yes," answered Mackeller, and being made reckless by example, he wrote a more lengthy message than was customary with him:

"Everything going on well here. The cooking I am doing consists in the production of hardbake cake, and the receipt is as follows: Take ore from Africa, salt and pepper to suit the taste, mix it with hard coal from the north, quick fire and a hot oven. When completely baked run into molds of sand, and place in a deep cellar to cool. Save the money you are wasting on the postoffice department by sending me, through parcel post, the cook book from which you are stealing those items, and use a telegram to let me know what has happened to the *Rajah* and Captain Wilkie."

In the evening an answer came.

"That's not a bad receipt of yours, Mackeller. I didn't think so serious a man as you was capable of such frivolity. The *Rajah* is in

Chancery, in litigation, in irons, in Plymouth harbor, in-junctioned. I expect it will be a long time before the *Rajah* gets out of court. Captain Wilkie is all right, and back on my yacht. The *Wychwood*, with Simmons in command, is off to Paramakaboo. I expect to be with you after you have had time to study the volume which at your suggestion I send to-day by parcel post; 'Mrs. Beeton's Book of Household Management'; bulky but useful."

Lord Stranleigh did not return, however, as promised, to the Cornish mine. Although apparently leading an aimless life at home, or in one or other of his clubs, or at an interesting race meeting, he was keeping his eye on Schwartzbrod by means of an efficient secret agent. He wondered how soon so shrewd a man as the financier would come to the knowledge that the *Rajah* was tied up with the red tape of the law, as immovable in her berth as if she had been chained to the breakwater by cables of steel. He was determined that Schwartzbrod should not further complicate the situation by sending out another steamer on an ore-stealing expedition to West Africa; and when at last he received a report from his agent that Schwartzbrod's men were in negotiation once more with Sparling & Bilge of Southampton, the indolent young man thought it time to strike, so he telephoned to Schwartz-brod, asking him to call at his town house next morning at half past ten, bringing his check book with him.

Schwartzbrod, spluttering at his end of the telephone, wished further explanation about the request for the check book. The charter money, he said, was not due. Nothing had been said in the document signed about payment in advance, but Stranleigh rang off, and left the financier guessing. When, some minutes later, Schwartzbrod got once more into communication with the house, the quiet-voiced Ponderby told him that his lordship had left for his club, but would expect to see him promptly at half past ten next day.

When Schwartzbrod arrived, he was shown this time into Lord Stranleigh's scantily furnished business office on the ground floor. He had been so anxious to know what the cause of the summons was that he found himself ten minutes before the half hour, and that ten minutes he spent alone in the little room. As the clock in the hall chimed the half hour, the door opened, and Lord Stranleigh entered.

"Good morning, Mr. Schwartzbrod. There are several little business matters which I wish to discuss with you and, as I expect to leave London shortly, I thought we might as well get it over." Stranleigh sat down in a chair on the opposite side of the table from the keen-eyed city man, who watched him with furtive sharpness.

"As I was telling you, my lord, there is nothing in the papers you signed saying that any payment was to be made in advance on account of the *Rajah*."

"You object, then, to paying in advance?"

"I don't object, my lord, if it's any accommodation to you. The first payment, you see, was made to Messrs. Sparling & Bilge."

"Of course, I've nothing to do with that."

"Well, the second amount I did not expect to be called on to pay until the steamer had earned some money."

"Ah, yes, I see. That seems quite just. The steamer, then, hasn't been earning money, I take it."

"It is too soon yet to say, my lord, whether she is earning money or not."

"Is she still at South America?"

"Yes, my lord."

"Has she not returned since I saw you last?"

"No, my lord."

"That's very strange," murmured Stranleigh, more to himself than to the other. "Shows how blooming inaccurate those newspapers are."

He took out from his inside pocket a thin memorandum book, searched slowly among some slips of loose paper, and at last took out a cutting from some daily journal.

"The paper from which I clipped this was issued a day or two after we last met. My attention was called to the item by the fact that so shortly before we had been in negotiation regarding the *Rajah*;

successful and pleasant negotiation, if I remember rightly, and I signed the papers you presented to me without consulting a solicitor, and the impression left on my mind is that you went away satisfied."

"Oh, I was perfectly satisfied, my lord, perfectly satisfied. Yes, you very kindly signed the renewal of the charter."

"You said, if I remember rightly, that the trip of the *Rajah* was merely an experiment. It had something to do with the cattle business; a ranch, or several ranches, in the Argentine Republic."

"Quite right, my lord. I regret to say the business has not been as prosperous as I had hoped."

"I am sorry to hear that. I have always looked on ranching as a sure way to wealth, but it seems there are exceptions. Now, you said to me that if the experiment did not prove successful, which, regrettably, seems to be the case, you would turn the *Rajah* over to me when she returned."

"But she has not returned, my lord."

"Then what does this journal mean by stating that a few days after we foregathered in this house the *Rajah* arrived at Plymouth from Brest, in France?"

"That must be a mistake, my lord. Would you let me read the item?"

Schwartzbrod extended his hand, trembling slightly, and took the slip of paper, adjusting his glasses to see the better, visibly gaining time before committing himself further.

"The item is very brief," commented Stranleigh, "still, it is definite enough. 'Steamer *Rajah*, Captain Wilkie, arrived at Plymouth from Brest.'"

"That cannot have been our *Rajah*," said Schwartzbrod at last, having collected his wits. "The captain on your steamer, my lord, is named Simmons."

"Simmons? Oh, Captain Simmons of Southampton? Why, I know the man. A fine, bluff old honest tar, one of the bulwarks of Britain. So Simmons was the captain of the *Rajah*, was he? Still, he may have resigned."

"He couldn't resign in midocean, my lord."

"Oh, I've known the thing done. I've known captains transferred from one steamer to another on the high seas."

"I've never heard of such a thing, my lord, unless one vessel was disabled, and then abandoned when another came along."

"My dear Mr. Schwartzbrod, accept my assurance that these daring devils of sea captains do things once they are out of our sight which we honest men ashore would not think of countenancing."

"I thought you said just now they were the bulwarks of Britain?"

"So they are, so they are, but bulwarks, Mr. Schwartzbrod, need to be made of stouter and coarser timber than that which lines the cabin. You must not think I am attributing anything criminal to our captain, Mr. Schwartzbrod; not at all, but it has often seemed to me that they do not always pay that scrupulous attention to the law which animates our business men in the city of London, for instance. A captain out of the jurisdiction of England, much as it may shock you to hear it, will dare to do things that would make our hair stand on end, and send a lawyer or a judge into a dead faint. Now, there's the Captain Simmons, of whom you just spoke. He tells me that he has undertaken devilish deeds in out-of-the-way parts of the world which he would not think of doing under that arch in the main street of Southampton."

The company promoter moistened his lips, and stroked the lower part of his face gently with his open hand. Lord Stranleigh beamed across at him with kindly expectancy, as if wishing some sympathetic corroboration of the statements he had made. At last the city man spoke.

"You have perhaps had more experience with seafaring people than I, my lord. I had always supposed them to be a rough-and-ready sort of folk, as reasonably honest as the rest of us."

"It was to be expected, Mr. Schwartzbrod, that your kind heart would hesitate to credit anything condemnatory said about them. Because you would not do this or that, you think other people are equally blameless. Take Captain Simmons, for instance, and yet, when I think of him I remember, of course, there were mitigating circumstances in the case. Captain Simmons had set his eye on a little bit of property, something like five acres, stretching down to Southampton water. There was a cottage and a veranda, and the veranda seemed to lure Captain Simmons with its prospect of peace, as he passed up Southampton water in command of the disreputable old *Rajah*. But Simmons never could succeed in saving the money to buy this modest homestead, but at last far more than the money necessary was offered him if he did a certain thing. It was a bribe, Mr. Schwartzbrod, and perhaps at first he did not see where he was steering the blunt snout of the old *Rajah*. He did not completely comprehend into what miasmatic and turbid waters his course would lead him. But when at last he saw it was involving him in theft, in wholesale robbery, and in potential murder, in the sinking of ships, and the drowning of crews, Simmons drew back."

A gentle expression of concern came into Lord Stranleigh's face as he saw the man before him in visible distress, sinking lower and lower in his chair. His face was ghastly: only the eyes seemed alive, and they were fixed immovably on his opponent, striving to penetrate at the thought or the knowledge that might be behind the mask of carelessness he wore.

"Don't you feel well, Mr. Schwartzbrod? Would you like a little stimulant?"

Without waiting for an answer he rang the bell.

"Bring some whisky and soda," he said, "also a decanter of brandy."

Schwartzbrod took a cautious sip or two of the weaker beverage.

"Were any names mentioned?" he asked.

"Simmons told me the tempter was a city man; some rank scoundrel who wished to profit by another's loss, and did not hesitate at robbery so long as he was legally safe in London, and others were taking the risk. They were to take the risk, and he was to secure the property. I even doubt if he intended to give the recompense he had promised. It amounted in Simmons's case to nine thousand pounds, and only one thousand was needed for the purchase of the place on which he had set his heart."

"But Simmons must have known, if such a sum was offered him, that he was undertaking a shady transaction?"

"That's exactly what I told him, but, you see, he had committed himself before he realized what he was letting himself in for. 'Chuck the whole business,' I said to him. 'You've got friends enough who'll buy that little place and present it to you. I am willing myself to subscribe part of the money,' and so Simmons struck. He is off, I understand, on another steamer. He has influential friends who got him a better situation than the one he held. Now, as I have said, I am willing to put some money on the table to buy that little house near Southampton. How much will you give, Mr. Schwartzbrod?"

Schwartzbrod now took a gulp of the whisky and soda. His courage was returning.

"Do you mean to tell me, Lord Stranleigh, that you have called a busy man like me to the West End in order to ask him for a charity subscription?"

"But surely you subscribe to many charities, Mr. Schwartzbrod?"

"I do not. It's as much as I can do to keep my own head above water, without troubling with other people. I believe in being just before being generous. If I pay my debts, that's all any man can ask."

"Most true philosophy, Mr. Schwartzbrod, but a little hard, you know. Some poor fellows get under the harrow, and surely we may stop our cultivation for a moment, and lift the harrow long enough to allow him to crawl out."

Schwartzbrod finished the whisky and soda, but made no further comment.

"It was not altogether for charitable purposes that I requested the pleasure of your call. There is business mixed with it. But you, Schwartzbrod, try to place the worst side of yourself before the world. You are really a very generous man. At heart you are; now, you know it."

"I don't know anything about it, my lord, and I do not understand the trend of this conversation."

"Well, I have come to the conclusion that you are one of the most generous men in London. You have done things that I think no other business man in London would attempt. You do good by stealth, and blush to find it fame, as I think the poet said. You've been doing me a great benefit, and yet you've kept quiet about it."

"What do you mean?"

"Why, I mean Frowningshield and his hundred and fifty men on my gold reef."

"What!" roared Schwartzbrod, springing to his feet.

"The kidnapping of Mackeller I did not mind. That's all in the day's work, and a mining engineer must expect a little rough and tumble in this world."

"I had nothing to do with that, my lord."

"No, it was Frowningshield who did it. Am I not saying that you are perfectly blameless? When I learned about the *Rajah's* expedition, about the money offered to Captain Simmons, about the compensation that was to be given to Frowningshield, about the running of the ore to Lisbon; when I heard all this, so prejudiced was my brain that I said to myself: 'Here I've caught the biggest thief in the world.' But when I learned that you had done it, I saw at once what your object was. You were going to smelt that ore without expense to me, take it over in ingots to England, and say, 'Here, Lord Stranleigh, you're not half a bad sort of chap. You don't understand anything about mining or the harsh ways of this world. Here is your gold.'"

Schwartzbrod poured down his throat a liquor glass full of brandy, and collapsed in his chair.

"You see, Mr. Schwartzbrod, there were only two alternatives for a poor brain like mine to accept: first, that you are the most generous man in the world; second, that you are the most daring robber in the world. Do you think I hesitated? Not for a moment. I knew you were no thief. Thieves are in Whitechapel, and Soho, and the East End generally, but not in the City of London. They're all men of law there. You are not a thief, are you, Mr. Schwartzbrod? No. Then sit down, honest man, and write me a check for the nine thousand pounds I have already paid to Captain Simmons, and for the amount which you promised to Frowningshield. I accept the benefit of your generosity in the same spirit in which it is tendered. I do not ask you where the gold is, I'll look after that; but the new ship you are trying to charter must not sail for the Paramakaboo. I cannot accept further kind offices from you. All I ask of you is to write a check for such an amount that it will fulfill the promises you made to Simmons and Frowningshield. That's why I requested you to bring your check book."

Schwartzbrod, with a groan, sat down at the table and drew forth his check book.

CHAPTER X—THE MEETING WITH THE GOVERNOR OF THE BANK

THE mere accumulating of money does not call for a high, order of intelligence. A stealthy craft is more valuable in that business than the intellect of a Shakespeare. The low cunning of a fox is often successful where the brave strength of a lion fails. Of course there are estimable men who accumulate a fortune through manufactory, discovery, or invention: men who are benefactors to their fellow creatures, and to whom money comes through the fruition of their endeavors to enrich the world rather than themselves. But a Stock Exchange speculator like Schwartzbrod, equipped with the sneaking slyness of an avaricious but ignorant peasant, becomes a mere predatory beast, producing nothing; fattening on the woes and losses of others; stealthy and cruel as the man-eating tiger. It is probable that as civilization advances such a vampire will be secluded from his fellows as the leper is in Eastern lands.

Since his first disastrous encounter with Lord Stranleigh, Schwartzbrod had been animated by a vicious hatred of this seemingly happy-go-lucky young man, whose attention appeared to be concentrated mainly on dress, but as they met again and again, this rancor became tinctured with a slowly rising fear, not of the urbane nobleman's intellect, but of his amazing good luck, for nothing could have persuaded Schwartzbrod that Stranleigh possessed intellect of any kind. He regarded this junior financier merely as a polite but brainless fop. To one as rich as Schwartzbrod, the writing of a check to fulfill his promises to Captain Simmons and Frowningshield should have been scarcely more important than the tossing of a penny to a beggar by an ordinary man. But Schwartzbrod brooded over it, grit his teeth, and swore vengeance. Now, vindictiveness is a quality which does not pay. In our modern strenuous life the man who wastes thought on revenge runs a risk of falling behind in the procession, but in a time of crisis such deflection of thought upon trivialities, when all senses should be on the alert to prepare for the coming storm, may be fatal. Schwartzbrod was like a man in an open boat on the sea, with too much canvas spread, who, instead of casting his weather eye around the horizon, and shortening sail, was fuming because some one had spilled a cupful of water at the bottom of the boat, pondering over the method of mopping it up, and flinging the soaked rag in the face of him who had upset the cup. A financial typhoon was approaching which would unroof many a house in England and America before it had run its course. Shrewd navigators on the treacherous waters of finance were preparing to scud under bare poles until the clouds rolled by.

It may be admitted at once that Lord Stranleigh no more suspected what was coming than did Schwartzbrod himself, for, as his lordship frequently confessed, he did not understand these things. He had, without browbeating or recrimination, eliminated all chance of Schwartzbrod's further interference with his mine. Schwartzbrod knew that Lord Stranleigh was possessed of every fact in the case, and these facts, if brought forward in a court of law, might very well sequester the city financier in a prison for the rest of his life, and Stranleigh, quite correctly, counted on this fear restraining Schwartzbrod's hand.

The big steamer *Wychwood* passed unmolested from southern to northern seas and back again, and Mackeller's industrious smelters had tumbled down into the safe deposit some two thousand tons of solid gold.

It was when city men began to return from their summer holidays that a slight whisper floated round the halls of Mammon which sent a shiver up and down the backs of shrewd people here and there. The whisper was to the effect that the Bank of England was in trouble. On three separate occasions within as many weeks, the bank rate had been raised, and now stood at so high a figure that it threatened to check enterprise and speculation during the approaching autumn, when everyone had hoped business would mend in the city. Cautious bankers began calling in their loans, which is a bank's method of shortening sail. Ambitious projects were being abandoned here and there through fear of shortness of money. Companies whose promoters looked forward to a successful flotation before Christmas, were held over. Affairs in the city were stagnant, and weather-wise people feared worse was to come. About the beginning of October a sinister rumor went abroad, founded on a highly sensational article in a New York yellow journal. This rumor, on account of its origin, was discredited at first, but presently the world came to learn that there was too good a foundation for it. The New York paper said that as soon as the financial amateurs of the British Parliament had placed on the statute books an Act commanding the Bank of England by the first of January to maintain its gold reserve at a hundred million of pounds, a powerful syndicate of financial experts had been formed in Wall Street for the cornering of gold. Wheat had often been cornered, to the great benefit of some one individual either in New York or Chicago, and to the universal loss of a hungry world, but no one had hitherto attempted to corner gold. Wheat could not be produced at will. Once the sowing was done, the mathematicians could estimate very accurately, given a full crop, the maximum number of bushels of wheat likely to be placed on the market the coming autumn, and to this amount no man could add, because the production of wheat depended on the slow revolution of the seasons. With gold it was different: gold could be produced summer and winter, night and day, therefore no individual, be he as rich as Midas, and no syndicate, however powerful, had heretofore dared to attempt the cornering of gold. Wheat was consumed year by year, but gold was practically everlasting, preserved in the shape of ornaments, bullion, platé, and what not. Old coinage, minted centuries before the birth of Christ, was still in existence, and although a few grains of wheat grown in the time of the Pharaohs rested in the palms of certain mummies, the great bulk of year before last's wheat was already ground and baked and eaten. It would seem, then, that the boldest financial coup ever attempted had been successfully accomplished by the men of Wall Street. This, however, the New York paper pointed out, was not the case. Tremendous as might be the consequences of the corner, there was, after all, little risk to the operators. Gold, unlike wheat, was a staple commodity. Wheat rose and fell in price. Gold practically did not. These men had paid no exorbitant rates for gold, but merely kept silent, and through the help of their agents all over the world, they either secured actual possession of the available metal, or had obtained an option on it, which did not expire until June, while the Bank of England was compelled by the new law to acquire possession of at least a hundred million pounds sterling of gold on January the first. Even if the corner failed, this would entail no loss to the monopolists, because they possessed the actual metal for which everything is sold. No sensational fall in the price of gold could take place, as would have been inevitable in the case of wheat should the corner fail, while as a result of the hold-up, if the bank was forced to come to their terms, the profit to be divided would be enormous. It was also stated that the Wall Street men had secured bank notes and orders for gold upon the Bank of England which they would present at a critical moment, demanding the metal, thus facing this venerable institution with the drastic alternative of accepting their terms, or suspending payment. The *Times* in a leading article, intended to soothe the public mind, attempted to show that the proposed cornering of gold was impossible; that millions upon millions of hoarded gold would be brought out at the proper moment if enough were offered for it; that these millions were in the possession of people of whom Wall Street knew nothing and had no means of getting into touch with.

This article had some effect in staying the panic, or at least in postponing it. Those responsible for the management of the Bank of England kept silent, as is their usual course, and for a week it seemed, so great was the confidence of Englishmen in their most important financial institution, that nothing disastrous was about to happen. Then stocks of all kinds began to come down with a run. One important house failed, then another, and another, and another, and shrewd men realized that both England and America were face to face with the greatest financial disaster of modern times. It seemed that the punishment fitted the crime, because of the fact that in America, which originated the crisis, the panic was much more severe than in England, and throughout all the United States, especially in the West, there was a simultaneous denunciation of Wall Street, to which Wall Street, accustomed to popular ebullition, paid little attention.

In England meetings were held calling on the Government to rescind their bill, and give the bank more time, but, as was pointed out, the bank had not asked for time, and although the governor and directors were known to have been bitterly opposed to the bill, the

Government could scarcely with dignity offer relief where relief had not been sought.

Lord Stranleigh sat at ease in one of the comfortable leather-covered armchairs which helped to mitigate the austerities of life in the smoking room of the Camperdown Club. His attitude was one of meditation. The right leg was thrown over the left; his finger tips met together, and those rather fine, honest eyes of his were staring through the thin film of smoke, and apparently seeing nothing. One of the men who had successfully borrowed money from him the day before, and whose salutation Lord Stranleigh ignored, not on account of the borrowed money, but simply because he had not seen the borrower, remarked to some friends that Stranleigh thought he was thinking, which caused a laugh, as these people did not know that the same remark had been made many years before, and were also under the delusion that Stranleigh was incapable of thought.

The Camperdown Club, as everyone knows, is more celebrated as a center of sport than as a resort of business men, yet it has two or three of the latter on its very select list of members. One of these entered, paused at the door, and looked about him for a moment as if wishing to find a chair alone, or searching for some friend whom he expected to meet. This was Alexander Corbitt, manager of Selwyn's Bank, a smooth-faced, harsh-featured man, under whose direction this bank, although a private institution, stood almost as high in public estimation as the Bank of England itself. As Corbitt stood there, the dreamy nature of Lord Stranleigh's gaze changed into something almost approaching alertness.

"Corbitt," he said, "here's a chair waiting for you."

The banker, without hesitation, strode forward, and sat down. There was a certain definite directness about each movement of his body which contrasted strikingly with the indifferent, indolent air assumed by most of the members; a decisive man of iron nerve, even one who knew little of him might have summed him up.

"What will you imbibe?" asked Stranleigh.

"Nothing, thank you. I just dropped in at the club for a bite of dinner, and having a few moments to spare, will now indulge in one cigar; then I must return to the bank."

"What, at this hour of the evening? I thought banks closed at four o'clock, or is it three?"

"I expect to be there all night," said Corbitt, shortly, as he held a match to his cigar.

"I wanted to ask you a few questions."

"Ask them."

"You know I am as ignorant as a child of all matters pertaining to finance, high and low?"

"Yes, I know that."

"What's all this fuss about, Corbitt?"

"What fuss?"

"Why, the accounts I read in the evening papers, and the morning papers, too, for that matter. They say there's a panic in the city. Is there?"

The banker laughed a little; a low, harsh, mirthless laugh.

"Yes, there's a panic," he said. "You are not nipped in it, I hope. I was told you were dabbling in the city a while ago. Is that true?"

"Oh, merely a small flutter, Corbitt, on behalf of some friends of mine."

"Have you been speculating lately?"

"Oh, no. I possess neither the brains nor knowledge requisite for success in the city."

"Brains and knowledge are at a discount just now. What is needed is cash. The biggest fool with ready cash can do more at this moment than the wisest man with a world of knowledge."

"Then I'd better jump into the turmoil," said Stranleigh, smiling.

"Take my advice, and keep out of it. There are rocks ahead. I see by to-night's papers that Conrad Schwartzbrod has gone under, and has carried down with him six or seven men who are considered the most acute financiers in the city. In ordinary times their standing might be supposed unimpeachable."

"Schwartzbrod bankrupt! Then it must be a fraudulent bankruptcy, surely?"

"No, it isn't. Everything has been swept away. He's had no time to hedge, or you may depend upon it he would have done so."

"Corbitt, what's the cause of the whole thing? Can't a man of your powerful intellect make it plain as A B C to an infant of my caliber?"

"The cause is simple enough. It is the attempt to do the right thing in the wrong way. The cause is the Bank of England's Gold Reserve Act, passed last May, and coming into force on the first of January next year. This Act makes it obligatory on the Bank of England to hold a reserve of a hundred millions in gold, where formerly it has only held, say, thirty millions. Do you understand so far?"

"Yes, Corbitt, I do. In fact, I remember last May picking up by wireless telegraphy part of the speech of the Chancellor of the Exchequer on this very bill, but I didn't understand it then, and don't now."

"Very well, the object which the Act sought to attain is one I have advocated for ten years past, but the way of accomplishing it is another instance of the conceited folly of a democracy meddling in a science that demands years of training and minds of a certain caliber. A democracy thinks that the right way to do a thing is the method adopted in bringing down the walls of Jericho. They beat drums and blow trumpets, and march round and round. Now, the exasperating feature of this case is that the Chancellor of the Exchequer knew at the time the folly of his own action, although, of course, he did not perceive the tremendous disaster it was going to bring upon not only his own country, but practically all the solvent nations of the world. He should have withstood the pressure of his unreasonable and ignorant followers. He should have arranged an interview with the managers of the Bank of England; should have told them that a bill of this kind was inevitable if they did not themselves put their house in order. He should have arranged with them quietly, without any beating of tom-toms, and blowing of horns, for the bank slowly to accumulate the needed reserve. Then he should have got up in his place in Parliament, and announced that the Bank of England already held the amount in gold which all thoughtful financiers believed to be necessary if we are to get rid of this eternally fluctuating bank rate.

"Of course, the Bank of England itself is also to blame; it being for all practical purposes a branch of the Government. It should have requested an interview, and come to some understanding before the bill passed into law. I expected that the lords would throw it out, and perhaps they thought the same. However, it passed both houses, received royal assent, and then the mischief was done. These very clever Wall Street men at once saw the possibilities of the situation, as they do with all amateur legislation. The bank remained silent and solemn; has given no word to this day, and then, at too late an hour, showed its distress by raising its bank rate again and again and again, hoping that would prove a magnet to attract gold, whereas it was merely hoisting a signal of distress, and acquainting the whole world with the fact it is drifting on a lee shore."

"Do you mean to say, Corbitt, that there's a chance of the Bank of England stopping payment?"

"No, I do not go so far as that. Here we come to the comic element of the tragedy, which shows the loose folly with which these Parliamentary bills are drawn. There is no penalty attached to the Act; it merely orders the bank to provide such a reserve by such a date. But if the bank doesn't do it, there can be neither a fine inflicted, nor can the governor be put into prison for contumely. If I were governor of the Bank of England, I would snap my fingers at Parliament, at the Act, and at the gold-cornering syndicate. I should say that as soon as was convenient to me I would accumulate this reserve of a hundred million, but that such action was impossible in the time given, therefore I should make no attempt to comply with the Act at the present moment."

"What would be the result of such a statement on the part of the governor?"

"I don't know. It would probably have a quieting result; or it might further accentuate the panic. Of course, when the governor began to perceive that it was going to be difficult to get the gold, he should have approached Parliament while it was in session, and got a relief bill, postponing the date, say for another year, but, as I have, said, he stood on his dignity; the Government stands on *its* dignity, and between the two of them they bring unnecessary ruin and disaster upon the country."

"Isn't it possible the bank will get the seventy extra millions by the first of January?"

"I see no possibility of it, unless they are prepared to pay two hundred millions for the accommodation to the Wall Street syndicate."

"Has the Wall Street syndicate got the gold? That is, the actual coin?"

"Yes, and showing its confidence, the money is actually in vaults here in London, so the syndicate seems to have no fear that our Government will commandeer the gold as Kruger did before the Transvaal War began. I understand that the syndicate has notified the Bank of England that the price of this metal will rise two hundred thousand pounds each day until the bank accepts their proposals."

"Corbitt, must the gold held in reserve by the Bank of England be in actual sovereigns, or raw metal?"

"Either one or the other."

"Suppose on the first of January the governor of the Bank of England were to announce that there are a hundred million pounds worth of gold in his vaults. What would be the effect on the country?"

"Stranleigh, there's more in that question than perhaps you think. I have never been just absolutely certain that you are as ignorant as you pretend. Most men in the city would tell you that such an announcement might instantly relieve the crisis, but if nothing were said until the first of January, and the announcement made then, I am not sure but it would be almost as disastrous as the former panic. It would be like the sudden releasing of a powerful and compressed spring, and anything sudden and powerful is apt to disarrange machinery. I think the inevitable result would be the instant soaring of stocks to much beyond their actual value. That, then, would bring ruin to many of those that had been spared by the fall of stocks. We should have a very disturbed market until things subsided to their proper level. And now you will have to excuse me, Stranleigh. I must be off."

The banker threw away the stub of his cigar, and marched out. Lord Stranleigh went over to one of the tables, and wrote several letters. Among them was a request for an interview at an early date sent to the governor of the Bank of England. Another was an order forwarded to Peter Mackeller in Cornwall. A third requested the honor of a meeting with Mr. Conrad Schwartzbrod. Then Stranleigh took the calendar of the dying year, and slowly counted the number of days remaining to its credit.

"I think there will be time enough," he said to himself, as he completed the count.

Four days after the lesson he had received on the crisis Lord Stranleigh kept the first appointment he had made by meeting Schwartzbrod in the little business office of the town house. The young man was shocked at the appearance of the aged financier, and, much as he disliked him, could not but feel sorry for him. He seemed almost ten years older than when last they met. His face was haggard, drawn, pinched; his shoulders stooping under the increased burden which misfortune had laid upon them. The only unchanged feature was his eyes, and from them gleamed the baleful light of unconquerable hate.

"I received your letter from the club," Schwartzbrod began. "I have come, you see, I have come. I am not afraid to meet you; you smooth, brainless sneak, you can do me no further harm. You have done your worst, and if you have called me here to triumph over me, I give you that pleasure, and freely acknowledge that you are the cause of all my misfortunes."

"I beg your pardon, Mr. Schwartzbrod, but you are quite mistaken in what you say. The cause of your misfortune goes farther back than any action of mine. The beginning was on the day when you resolved to crush the Mackellers. They had helped you, father and son. They were innocent men, and honest. Each in his own way had assisted you to the possibility of almost unlimited wealth. That did not satisfy you. You determined to take from them their just compensation, and to fling them, paupers, into the gutter. It happened through one of those freaks of fate which keeps alive our faith in eternal justice, that the day you came to this resolve you were a doomed man."

"That's what you called me here to tell me, is it, you human poodle dog, you contemptible puppy, rich through the thefts of your ancestors."

"Your language, Mr. Schwartzbrod, seems to have become tinged with the intemperance of the panic. I did not intend to refer to the past at all. You set the subject of our conversation the moment you entered the room, and I merely followed your lead, and strove to remove a misapprehension from your mind as to the original causes of things. No, my invitation to this house had quite another object. I shall not strain your credulity by asking you to believe that when I heard four days ago you were bankrupt, a feeling of slight regret was uppermost in my mind. I don't like to see people suffer."

The old man laughed, like the grating of a file on a saw.

"Of course I don't ask you to believe that, and should be sorry to put such a strain on whatever belief in human nature you may possess, so don't trouble any further about my statements, which you doubtless regard as absurd. Have you got any money left?"

"Not a stiver."

"How about your six colleagues; are they cleaned out?"

"Even if they had money, they would not intrust a penny of it to me. You talk about my belief in human nature. Well, the faith in human nature in me is gone. I have done my best for them, and lost every point in the game, together with their money and my own."

"Very well, Mr. Schwartzbrod, we must rehabilitate you. I possess what I think is the finest red automobile in London, and my chauffeur would add dignity to the equipage of an emperor. I will lend you chauffeur and car for the day, and if you drive through the streets round the bank for a few hours, those who turn up their noses at you will be lifting their hats instead."

"I suppose you think that's funny, Lord Stranleigh. You wish to exhibit me in your motor car after the fashion of the Romans parading their captives in their chariots when defeated. I don't know why I came here, but I warn you I did not come to be insulted."

"Of course not. It is incredible you should imagine it possible for me to insult a man in my own house. Now listen to me. My banker has asked as a favor that I should not draw any checks upon him until this flurry is over. Of course, if I did draw a check, he would honor it, but I have given him my promise. Under the back seat of this automobile I have hid away eight bars of gold, each weighing a hundred pounds or thereabout, and valued probably at five thousand pounds sterling. That means forty thousand pounds in exactly the commodity all London is howling for at the present moment. I don't know precisely what the position of a bankrupt is, and it may be possible that your creditors can take away those bars of gold if they knew you possessed them, therefore trade in my name if you like; act as my agent. Go in this automobile to your bank, and get the porters to carry the bullion inside. There they will weigh it, and estimate its value, giving you the credit for the amount. Now, pay strict attention to me. Buy the value of those bars in stocks which you know possess some intrinsic worth, but are now far beneath their proper level. Hold those stocks until the first of January, when you will see begin the greatest boom that London has ever known. I advise you to sell as soon after New Year's day as possible, because stocks are likely to shoot up to a higher point than they may be able later to maintain. This gold comes from a mine which was once in your possession, and my immature puppy mind is so absurdly constructed that I have felt uneasily in your debt for a long time, and now am glad of the opportunity to allow you a share in the prosperity of the mine, if you will be obliging enough to accept it."

The truculence of the ruined financier immediately fell from him at the mention of gold, and in its place came the old cringing manner, with a flattering endeavor to mitigate the harshness of his former remarks, a change of manner that made the young man shrink a little farther from him, and hurriedly end the interview.

"That's all right, Mr. Schwartzbrod. Words break no bones, unless they cause the recipient to fling the dealer in them down a steep stairway. The automobile is waiting for you at the door. The chauffeur thinks the metal under the seat is copper. Your banker will tell you it is gold, so keep an eye on it till it is safely in his possession. There, there, do not thank me, I beg of you. I assure you I am not seeking for gratitude, but I am a little short of time to-day. In half an hour I am to meet the governor of the Bank of England, so I must bid you farewell."

"Will you not come with me, then, in your own automobile, my lord?"

"Thank you, no. I think it best that you should be seen alone in the automobile if there have been rumors regarding your position down in the city. If anyone asks you what the machine cost, you can tell them its price is a net two thousand pounds. You will journey in that, and I shall take the twopenny tube, being a democratic sort of person. Good morning, Mr. Schwartz-brod, good morning."

So Lord Stranleigh went down the huge lift at the twopenny tube, and in due time emerged to daylight at the Bank of England. He arrived in the anteroom a few minutes before the time of his appointment, and exactly at the arranged moment was called for, and ushered into the presence, for punctuality is the politeness of kings, and—governors of the Bank of England.

The stern, almost commanding attitude of this monarch of finance abashed the young man, and made him feel the useless worm of the dust Schwartzbrod had indicated he was. Stranleigh, who was always more scrupulously polite to a beggar than was his custom with the king, resented the sensation of inferiority which came upon him when confronted with the forbidding ruler of the bank. He said to himself:

"Good Heavens, is it possible that if I meet a man who is big enough, I shall actually cringe in my soul as Schwartzbrod does with his body?"

Nevertheless, that slight hesitation in speech which was apt to incommode him at critical moments overpowered him now, and his dislike of any attempt to win the respect of the iron man before him sent him in the other direction, and he knew that for the next ten minutes he was going to be regarded as the most hopeless fool in London. Yet he did not consider himself a fool, and his latent sense of humor prevented him from making any attempt at endowing his conversation with that wisdom which seemed so suitable to this somber room.

When the governor's secretary had presented Lord Stranleigh's letter to him, the head of the bank had peremptorily refused to waste time with a member of the aristocracy of whom he knew nothing, but the secretary, whose business it was to know everything, dropped one word in a short phrase that arrested the governor's attention.

"It's the *rich* Lord Stranleigh, sir."

The word "rich" was the straw at which the drowning man clutched. So here was Stranleigh, the living contradiction of that phrase "The last of the Dandies." Here was the embodiment of the spirit of Piccadilly and Bond Street confronted with the rugged, carelessly dressed dictator of Threadneedle Street, a frown on the beetling brow of one man, an inane, silly smile on the lips of the other. At the sight of this smile the governor saw at once that his first thought had been right. He should not have wasted a moment on this nonentity, yet he had before him the herculean task of providing the institute over which he presided with seventy millions of pounds worth of gold within five days, or stand discredited before the world. Despair was strangling expiring hope as he realized that this simpering noodle could not be the god in the machine; godlike in stalwart form, perhaps, but that simpering smile would have discredited Jove himself.

"What can I do for you, my lord?" he bellowed forth, temper, patience, and time short.

"Well, sir," sniggered Stranleigh, "there's—there's several things you can do for me. In—in the first place you don't mind my sitting down, do you? It seems to me I can speak better sitting down. I've—I've really never been able to make a speech in my life, even after dinner, simply because a fellow has to stand up, don't you know."

"I hope, my lord, you won't think it necessary to make a speech here."

"No, no, I merely wished a quiet talk," said his lordship, drawing up a chair without invitation, and sitting down. "You see, I have no head for figures, and so little knowledge of business do I possess that

I am compelled to engage twelve professional men to look after my affairs."

"Yes, yes, yes, yes," snapped the governor.

"Well, you see, governor, now and again I act without asking any advice from those men. Seems kind of a silly thing to do, don't you think? Keeping twelve dogs, and barking a fellow's bally self, don't you know."

"Yes. What has all that to do with the Bank of England?"

"I'm coming to that. You see, we are all imbued with the same respect for the bank that we feel for the church, and the navy, and the king, and sometimes for the Government, but not always, as, for instance, when they pass silly Acts about your gold reserve, instead of coming to you in a friendly manner, as I'm doing, and settling the thing quietly."

"I quite agree with you, my lord, but my time is very limited, and I should be obliged— —"

"Quite so, sir, quite so. These ideas are not my own, at all. I didn't know much about the crisis until four or five days ago when Mr. Corbitt—Alexander Corbitt, you know, of Selwyn's Bank. You're acquainted with him, perhaps?"

"I know Mr. Corbitt—yes."

"Well, those are his opinions, and I agree with him, you know."

"Mr. Corbitt is an authority on finance," admitted the governor, as if, instead of praising the absent man, he was denouncing him.

"Now, what bothers me about gold is this. A sovereign weighs a hundred and twenty-three grains, decimal—well I forget the decimal figures, but perhaps you're up in them. I never could remember—to tell you the truth, the moment I get into decimals, I'm lost. I can figure out that two and two are four, but beyond that— —"

"I assure you, my lord," interrupted the governor, "a great many people cannot go so far as that. If you will have the kindness, not to say the mercy, to tell me exactly what you want, I will guarantee that your answer will be brief and prompt."

"All right. To get directly at the nub of the business, then, do you have twelve ounces to the pound of gold, or sixteen?"

The governor's fingers were drumming on the hard surface of the table. He glared at his visitor, but said nothing.

"When I get entangled with decimals or vulgar fractions, it's bad enough, but when I don't know whether the pounds I am dealing with are twelve ounces or sixteen ounces, then the ease gets kind of hopeless—ah, I see you are in a hurry. Now tell me how much would be the value of a bar of gold weighing a hundred pounds, and we'll let troy or avoirdupois go. Just give me a rough estimate."

"My Lord Stranleigh," said the governor, with ominous calmness, "have you come here under the impression that the Bank of England is an infant school?"

Lord Stranleigh blushed a delicate pink, until his cheeks were as smooth and crimson as that of a girl receiving her first proposal. The contempt of the man before him was so unconcealed that poor Stranleigh thought, as he closed his open hand, he might feel it, so thick was it in the air. He plunged desperately into another tack.

"My dear governor," he stammered, trying to conciliate his opponent by cordial familiarity, "as I told you I have the utmost respect for the Bank of England. You see, I am rather well off, and within the last day or two I have plunged, and every available asset I possess except one I have put into stocks and shares. I've thought this thing out— —"

"Oh, you've thought it out," said the governor.

"Yes, as well as I was able, and I believe that after the first of January London is going to see the greatest boom in stocks and shares that has ever taken place in the history of finance."

"What are your grounds for such a belief, my lord?"

"The—the respect I hold for the Bank of England. We want to see the good old Bank of England buck up. It's humiliating to think that an upstart like Wall Street should be able to play Hey-diddle-diddle, the cat and the fiddle, with a venerable institution like this. Why, it's as if some one spoke disrespectfully of one's grandmother. I want to see the bank buck up, and that's why I'm here."

The governor bucked up. He rose like a statue of wrath.

"My lord, this interview must terminate. The Bank of England cannot assist you in your speculations. You should have consulted Alexander Corbitt if you wished further credit, should he happen to be your banker."

Stranleigh had risen when he saw the governor on his feet.

"I did."

"Then you had better go back to him. He surely never advised you to see me?"

"No, but what he told me of the situation filled me with a desire to meet you."

"I dare say. Well, Lord Stranleigh, you have met me. I bid you good morning, sir."

Stranleigh became a deeper crimson at what he considered this rude dismissal. He was not accustomed to being treated in such a way. His shoulders squared back, and the smile left his lips.

"Then you don't want the gold?" he said, almost as sternly as the other had spoken.

"What gold?"

"My gold."

"I thought you said that all your assets had been vested in the buying of stocks."

"I said, sir, all my assets except one. The one asset remaining is gold."

"Gold?"

"Yes."

"In what form?"

"In the form of ingots."

"How much gold have you got? What's its value?"

"Now, governor, I put it to you, as one man to another, you're a little unreasonable. Didn't I tell you that unless I can multiply a hundred and twenty-three decimal-whatever-it-happens-to-be, I can't even estimate it? I asked—I hope with courtesy—the favor of your assistance in calculating the value of my gold, but you began to talk about infant schools. You see, I have got a mine down in Cornwall that holds two thousand tons of gold."

"Nonsense," interrupted the governor, waxing impatient. "There are no gold mines in Cornwall."

"Sir, I did not say there were. The mine I speak of is a copper mine."

"I have had enough of this fooling, my lord, and I think I have already bade you farewell."

"Then you don't want my gold?"

"How many pounds of raw gold have you got?"

"Pounds? Oh, I don't estimate my gold in pounds. I hold at present upward of two thousand tons."

"Two thousand tons! In ore, do you mean?"

"Certainly not. If the Bank of England is not an infant school, I suppose it is not a smelting furnace, either. This gold, as I told you, has been smelted, and is in ingots. I came down by twopenny tube to keep my appointment because I had lent my principal automobile to a man named Conrad Schwartzbrod. I see my automobile standing outside, and as I gave Schwartzbrod eight bars of this metal, telling him to take it to his bank, he seems to have taken it to this bank, so if this seminary for young ladies has purchased these eight bars, we may go at once and examine them. My two thousand tons is divided into ingots similar to those Schwartzbrod has sold you."

"Where is your gold?"

"A thousand tons of it is in Cornwall still, but can be delivered here within a day or two. The other thousand tons is on a special train of the Great Western Railway, which has already arrived in London, and its contents may be in your vaults this evening if your vans look sharp."

The governor sat down in his chair more hurriedly than he had anticipated, drew out a handkerchief and wiped his brow.

"Are you telling the truth, or is this—is this—What you say, my lord, is incredible."

"Very well, come up to the Great Western goods depot, and see for yourself. I have always avoided the city as a cynical place, but I had no idea that unbelief was so prevalent there as it seems."

"A thousand tons of gold! Worth a hundred and ten million pounds sterling!"

"There, you see how easy it is to calculate when a man who knows figures gets at it. Is that what my thousand tons is worth?"

"Where did this gold come from?"

"From the West African coast; a very valuable surface mine I own there. We've been working most of the year transporting the ore to Cornwall and smelting it, tossing the ingots down into an empty copper mine I own, which I call my safe deposit vault."

"How much do you demand for this gold?"

"Oh, I don't demand anything at all. I'm no business man, as I told you. It struck me that the gold was quite as safe in your vaults as in my copper mine, therefore I engaged a special train to bring half of it up. You can have the other half if you wish."

"My lord, will you accompany me in my automobile to the Great Western goods depot, and show me that special train of yours?"

"Governor, I shall be delighted."

A few mornings later Lord Stranleigh sat at his appetizing breakfast, and smiled as he read the leading article in the *Times*:

"As our readers know, we did not join in the outcry of the sensational press which did so much to mislead public opinion both in England and America. Never for an instant, during all the tumult, did our faith in that greatest and most venerable of financial institutions, the Bank of England, waver. On October the fourteenth we pointed out the impossibility of cornering gold, no matter how powerful the financial syndicate might be which undertook his labor of Sisyphus. How long this treasure, whose very figures read like some romance of the 'Arabian Nights,' has lain in the vaults of the bank, no one but the governor, and those in his confidence, can tell. While the country was ringing with predictions of failure on the part of the bank to conform with a new and absurd law, those responsible for the direction of our leading financial institution quietly and in silence had gathered together the almost unimaginable amount of three hundred million pounds' worth sterling of virgin gold. Those journals which for the past four months have been foremost in deluding their readers, and bringing a crisis on the country, are now loud in their denunciation of the governor of the bank for not speaking sooner. But if the governor of the bank undertook to reply to statements, malicious or ignorant, concerning the institution over which he so worthily presides, there would be little time left for him to perform those functions that he has so ably accomplished. Those people who held faith in their country are rewarded. The almost unprecedented heights to which stocks and shares have risen means the enrichment of every investor who was not carried away by a senseless panic. As for ourselves, we have in season and out of season never swerved from——"

Lord Stranleigh laughed.

"Good old Times," he said, "how wise you are! A fitting companion grandmother to the Old Lady of Threadneedle Street!"

THE END

CPSIA information can be obtained
at www.ICGtesting.com
Printed in the USA
BVHW031011280323
661284BV00009B/579